KISS A GINGER DAY

ELIZABETH SAFLEUR

Elizabeth SaFleur LLC
PO Box 6395
Charlottesville, VA 22906
Elizabeth@ElizabethSaFleur.com
www.ElizabethSaFleur.com

Edited by Olivia Kalb
Proofed by Claire Milto
Cover design by LJ Designs

ISBN: 978-1-949076-61-5

Glossary of Terms
(Welsh translated)

Ffyc = Fuck

Dwrn uffern = The sentiment similar to "fucking great"

Alice blinked snowflakes off her lids and cursed. Her stupid high heels kept sinking into the growing slush—and Theodore, a man she'd known for exactly two hours, would not stop with the questions. The last thing anyone wanted in a surprise Washington, DC winter storm was to play a get-to-know you game as a distraction.

She wanted the gloves and hat she'd left at the office.

She wanted an industrial-sized vat of coffee laced with amaretto.

But most of all, she wanted to find her damned car.

She glanced up and down the residential street. It looked familiar. Sort of.

"What did you say again?" She was only half listening to him spout off his favorite *everythings*.

So far, they'd covered favorite months, foods, movies— his was an action flick, of course—and which one of the seven dwarfs in *Snow White*. Hers was Doc. His? Happy.

He helped steady her as she almost slipped again. "My favorite month is January." The man whose sanity she was seriously questioning lifted his hand to catch some of the flakes that would not quit falling from the sky. The fact that he introduced himself to Alice at the party as "Theodore Gaston the Fourth, at your service" was a clue he might be a bit off.

But Theodore had a hypnotic British accent. It lured her into thinking he was safe. Plus, her work colleagues laughed with him all night across the bar. But within seconds of exiting the bar, he was peppering her with all these odd questions. "A game," he'd stated. "Something to make us forget the cold."

Instead, it made her question her choices—yet again. Why hadn't she paid closer attention to where she'd left her car? And why did she have to have one that still used a key? She'd kill for one of those fob things that beeped.

She slipped her half-frozen arm free of his. "Tell me one good thing about this month because we're out of *Christmas* January and now into *real* January."

"That's why. Holidays are over, pressure's off. No one cares what you're doing. Plus …" He dramatically stopped and swept his hands over his peacoat. "It has 'Kiss a Ginger' day."

"You made that up." Probably hoping she was into red-headed guys. He had to be trying to pick her up. Men didn't bolt from a party and offer to help you find your lost parked car in twenty-something degree weather for nothing.

"Not making it up," he said. "It's tomorrow, January 12. January 18 is Museum Selfie Day. January 23 is National Pie Day. There's Chinese New Year, Martin Luther King, Jr. Day. Oh, and damn, we missed National Bobblehead Day."

"Tragic."

"It is. It was January 7."

Oh, my God. What was she thinking, walking with a complete stranger on a deserted—and very snow-wet and chilly—street?

Maybe because tonight sucked, and the last thing she needed was to die of exposure and in some snow pile—alone. Blowing on her fingertips, she sighed.

Tonight, when her boss asked her to meet him at Harrison's Pub, she'd thought it was to discuss her promotion to CFO. Three months ago, the former CFO, Brian, quit in a huff. He didn't even tell her he was leaving, and they'd worked together for the last two years.

Roger immediately dangled the position in front of her. They'd had several private dinners to talk about it—"to avoid distractions, a relaxed conversation out of the office." Instead, tonight, he'd invited the entire office to the pub for a surprise birthday party for himself. Who did that?

But that wasn't the worst part. Apparently, he'd asked Tricia to write up a new CFO job description that week—something she'd found out when Stephanie and Tricia accosted her in the tiny ladies' room. "We feel bad you don't seem to understand. He was auditioning you for Miss December. That's what all those dinners were. We've seen it before."

They'd thought she and Roger had *dated*. And not only that, but that she'd been the potential flavor of the month. *Jesus*.

Right then, her New Year's Resolution was formed. She'd stop being so timid, and she'd take control of her destiny. It was important to pick one thing every year to improve about oneself.

But she'd stomped out of the party only to discover a blanket of snow over everything in sight. Pretty, but every single car on the street was a mound of white. So much for controlling her fate.

Following her out was Theodore. "Need help?" he'd asked in his lilting accent.

At the time, it had seemed smart to take him up on his

offer. He'd looked harmless enough. Then again, Ted Bundy and probably Jack the Ripper had as well. They'd turned out to be serial killers.

She quickened her pace, only to almost slip again. "Oof."

He grabbed her elbow. "Steady, there. High heels, huh?" There most definitely was a judgy look in his eyes.

"It was a workday," she huffed. She should have called a rideshare. If there were any to call. Washington, DC shuttered all activity when anything fell from the sky.

He dropped his hold on her elbow and moved to the outside of the street. "Now, your favorite month?"

"May. Flowers. Sunshine. So, where are you from exactly in England?"

"I'm not. From Wales." His coattails rose up as he reached for his wallet and drew out a driving license, holding it up to her face.

"Oh. You really are Theodore Gaston."

"Of course I am. Ah, you thought I was kittyfishing."

A little laugh bubbled up. "It's catfishing. And, yeah, of course, I did. I mean—" she waved in the direction of the bar behind them "—it's what half those people in there are doing."

"Well, I'm not anyone."

"No, you're Theodore Gaston *the Fourth*."

"Yeah, not my smoothest move to let that slip. I mean, you could be out for all my money and fame."

She stopped. Gazed at him. Was he famous, and she'd missed it? DC was filled with celebrities who walked among regular people like her.

He winked and pointed at her. "Gotcha. I'm as ordinary as the day is long."

"Not ordinary," she said. "Not if you're walking me to my car." Her last date had sat in his car, engine idling, and texted her he was "outside."

"That should be the most standard thing you experience."

She stared up at him. The guy couldn't be for real. For a long moment, she stood frozen, a little mesmerized by all the bright blue in his eyes.

A gust of cold air unstuck her gaze. "Thanks for helping me, Theodore." She shouldn't be looking a gift horse in the mouth. But once she was in her car, Theodore could go on his merry way. She was tired and cold, and she needed her stupid high heels *off.*

"Never a chore, always a pleasure, love."

A tingle ran down her spine at his charming talk. Again, it had to be the British accent because she was over not having common sense when it came to what people *really* wanted—especially those with a pair of testicles.

Eyes open. Control. That would be her mantra.

He stuffed his hands into the pockets of his jacket. "My mother would have my backside if I let a woman walk by herself in the dead of night."

Ah. Now, he made sense. The guy still lived in his mother's basement, didn't he? "Don't want to disappoint Mom."

"But I know what you're thinking."

"You must save a lot of money living with your parents?"

"Ha. Like my parents' place in Tenby Harbour has room for me. You're thinking, 'How is this handsome, single guy with the adorable accent all by himself on a fine January evening such as this'." His smile forced little crinkles to form around his blue eyes.

Her eyes nearly rolled to the back of her head. "I'm thinking I hope I have my toes at the end of this night." Her feet stung.

When they rounded the corner, she raised her arms and let them drop by her side. "I swear I parked on this street, but who could tell?"

"Tell you what. You stand under that shelter." He pointed

at an apartment building with a faded red awning and gold lettering announcing it as *The Paramount*. "I'll wipe off the cars, and you yell when one of them looks like yours."

"You'd do that?"

"Love, I wore boots. But you?" He pointed at her heels, now likely ruined. "The weather app is a wondrous invention."

"So I've heard." She slipped under the awning.

He dramatically wiped at the side of a car. "Ah, red sedan something. Yours?"

"Nope. My car is silver." She stomped her feet, hugging her arms around her body.

He dramatically skidded along the wet surface like a surfer, his arms swiping at the next car's hood at the same time. "Nope," he called out. "Blue."

His head swiveled to face her. "Is silver your favorite color?" His shout echoed on the abandoned street.

"Green."

"Mine, too. Imagine that." He stopped at another car and had to raise his voice more. "Okay. Favorite vacation spot."

"Not here," she mumbled. She glanced at the darkened townhouses lining the street. It appeared early-to-bed Washingtonians lived there. It was only eleven at night. "We should be careful to not wake people," she whisper-shouted.

"What?" he yelled. "Waikiki, you say?"

She drew out her phone. A rideshare *had* to be available. She tapped the app. Ninety minutes was the earliest anyone could get to her. She brought her phone up to her mouth. "Hey, Siri, call a taxicab."

And that was when her phone screen went black. Battery dead. Oh, for the love of…. Tonight had devolved into the ridiculous.

She strode, or rather slid, her way toward Theodore, who

was arm-brushing off a black Mercedes, the little emblem sticking out of its snow casing.

He waved over the Mercedes hood. "Man, this car is a boat."

"It's a lost cause, and I'm calling a cab. Can I borrow your cell?"

"Don't have one."

Momentary shock made her still. "You don't have a cell phone?" How did he live?

"Forgot it back at my place. We could go there, and—"

She raised a hand to stop his words. As if tonight could get any worse. She sucked in snow-humid, cold air, and heaved out a foggy breath. "There has to be a cab somewhere." She craned her neck up the street. So. Many. Snow. Mounds.

Her feet slipped once again, and her belly lurched. Strong arms banded around her, and suddenly, she was in his arms. Oh, hard chest.

"Come on, Snow Kitten, since you seem hellbent on finding your car, I'll carry you. You swipe at the cars until we uncover yours."

The evening truly was surreal. Laugher burst out of her chest as he hefted her in his arms. "Do you always sweep girls off their feet like this?"

"Only the beautiful ones with snow in their hair. Now, swipe." He leaned down, and she had to hook her arm around his neck to keep from being pitched over.

What the hell. It would be *wise* to accept help when needed. "I'm losing my mind," she muttered and swiped at a car hood—not hers.

They repeated the move on another car. Again, the wrong car.

He'd carried her as if she weighed as much as a dried flower. And he kept asking her questions, seemingly unbothered by the chilled air, though his cheeks and ears had reddened. His eyes grew impossibly bluer.

"Favorite holiday spot?" he asked.

"Australia."

"Ah, that country is lovely this time of year." He shifted her in his arms a little so she could lean down to swipe at what turned out to be a white sedan. "Especially Queensland. Fantastic beaches. I can see why down under would be your favorite."

She'd only been once but had fallen in love with it. "It really is something."

He continued to quiz her about her favorite things. Somewhere between her announcing Australia as her favorite place to visit and her favorite fabric—yes, he'd asked that question—she'd lost all inhibition about being carried by a strange man in a snowstorm. If nothing else, it'd make for a good story. In fact, she'd be sure to tell Stephanie and Tricia on Monday, and with any luck, it'd get back to Roger, her bastard boss.

She'd be extra dramatic about the details, too. How a handsome British man who clearly worked out regularly, given his breath remained steady despite his arms being full of her, came to her rescue and *helped*. Not offered false promotion promises.

That is, if they ever found her damned car and she made it to work tomorrow.

"Now, Alice, rapid fire round. Red or white wine?"

"Red." She'd love a glass right now, in fact.

"Picnic outside or sheepskin by the fireplace?"

"Picnic in May. Fireplace in January." She leaned her head back, gazing at the dark sky dotted by white flakes. It *was* pretty.

Sounds in the distance were muffled as if the world were wrapped in cotton. His footfalls softly creaked in the growing inches of snow. The soft plink-plink of snowflakes hitting the ground mixed with the sound of her breath. Even the beep-beep-beep of a truck in the distance was muted.

He shifted her a bit. "Jazz music or country?"

"Of those choices? Jazz."

"Oh, good." He smiled down at her. "Our first date is now planned."

"Oh, really?" She eyed him, bouncing a little in his arms. He most definitely worked out—a lot. "Have I landed in a Hallmark movie?"

"Sorry to disappoint, but I'm not a widow with a sheep farm-turned-lodge in Scotland or a lumberjack in Montana with a 20,000-acre ranch who's sworn off love until we lock eyes."

She laughed. "A fan, are you?"

His brow furrowed, and he shook his head. "Eh. Those guys are amateurs. But my mum regularly swoons over them. And you think it's cold here? Visit Scotland in January with a storm blowing in. Now, brush this one." He leaned over and she once more uncovered a car, not hers.

"Scotland is on my bucket list," she said.

"We can stay at Glenapp Castle."

Her heart hitched a little. "We?"

"Who's going to keep your heels dry?"

"I have boots," she sniffed.

"With heels?"

Busted. "I can get wellies."

"Ah, there's my girl." His smile grew wider.

She couldn't imagine what being his girl would entail. Endless questions. Chivalry. Travel. Nights of staring into his eyes, which were so blue it reminded her of those pictures of Broome, Australia, she had on her computer wallpaper. And even if he were peculiar, he seemed genuine.

"What kind of car do you drive anyway?" he asked, as they stopped at—what? Their twentieth car?

"A silver Audi." She leaned over and let her coat arm, now caked with snow, swipe on the hood—and bingo. "This one!" She began to wiggle out of his arms, and he mercifully steadied her as she dropped to her feet. She stumbled a little, given her ankles and feet were numb with cold.

She dug into her coat pocket and pulled out her key.

Note to self: buy a car with a very loud key fob chime sound.

Chivalrous Theodore held on to her as they rounded to the driver's side.

She got the door open with a loud crack. "You were a life-saver. Let me drive you to your car?"

"I'd be a fool to not take you up on it. And for the record, I know where my rental is."

She laughed, climbed inside and started up the car. He then proceeded to brush the snow off her car windows with this coat sleeve. The man most certainly didn't live there.

How often had she met someone who would spend thirty minutes with her like that? How about never?

Once he was in the passenger's side, the heat had begun to work. She wiggled her fingers in front of the vent sending blessed warm air her way.

"Okay, then." He yanked on his seat belt. "I'm the next block over."

"You're on Ordway?"

He cocked his head toward her. "Parked in front of the bar. As snowed in as anyone else by now, I suppose."

He could have driven away before there was a good eight inches of snow on the ground. "But … you'd said you wanted to share a cab." He also could have driven *her* home. Then again, she'd never have gotten into a stranger's car. Especially not now. She had a renewed commitment to keeping her eyes as wide open as the Grand Canyon.

He shrugged. "Wanted to make sure you got home safe first."

Oh. Her lips involuntarily parted, as she gaped at him. A warmth built inside her, melting a bit of her usual defenses against men who used pretty words—like whispered "promotion" to her but didn't mean it.

She angled herself so her back was against her car door. She was sure a logical question existed in her brain, her body, somewhere. She couldn't seem to form words to ask it. What did she want to know?

Was he playing her?

Was he that charming to every woman?

Did he just want to get laid?

Who cared? Tomorrow, she'd think long and hard about her recent choices.

She put her car in reverse to gain a few inches so she could get out of the parking space and avoid the other two snowed-in cars in front and behind her.

Of course, her wheels spun. And spun. And spun. They didn't move the car a millimeter.

"Oh, great." She dropped her forehead to her steering wheel. She did not have that—or any part of that night—on her evening's bingo card.

"Guess we might as well start that first date."

"Oh?" she asked, her face still buried in her steering wheel. "Got a bottle of red wine on you? And a fireplace?"

"No, but I've got one at my place a block over."

She twisted her face to stare at him, forehead still on the cold vinyl. "You live on Ordway, too?" She lifted her head and dropped it against the headrest. "Why didn't you save yourself? Why do all this?"

"To get to know you I'd have flown to Australia and back."

His eyes shone over at her, a half-smile camped on his lips. "But only in international business class. It's a really long trip."

When she didn't say anything, he mirrored her movement. He squared himself to her and took her fingers in one hand. "Okay, would you rather I said Scotland?" he asked seriously. "Because I could do either."

She shook her head. "You aren't real."

"I'm as real as the driven snow, love." He cracked open his door. "Come on, I'll even carry you to my flat. Unless you want to spend the night here."

Another stupid laugh erupted through her nose, and she repositioned herself to face the windshield. She would be a fool to go with him. But they were nowhere near a metro stop, and she hadn't seen a single car or taxi on the snow-laden street.

A blast of cold air hit her as he stepped out. "I promise you're safe with me."

"That's what serial killers say," she whispered to her steering wheel.

He leaned down, his face bright in the open door. "Not the ones Edison Tech hires. They understand the whole adage of 'you get what you pay for'. And I'd be too expensive."

"You don't work for Edison." She handled payroll. She'd know if they had a recent hire.

"Not technically, but I know some of the people there. So, about that wine?"

"Theodore …"

He shut her inside with the click of her passenger car door.

Wine did sound pretty great—definitely better than freezing to death overnight in her car. She could always call a cab—if any were running—from his place.

She yanked open her own door and stood. "Okay, take me to your alcohol."

His blue eyes glittered her way. "Good because in—" he checked his watch "—fourteen minutes, it will officially be Kiss a Ginger Day."

"As long as it's Cabernet Sauvignon Day somewhere." She wasn't interested in kissing anything except the rim of a wineglass—and maybe finding out who he knew at Edison. It always helped to network, and maybe he knew someone who needed a CFO.

2

———————

Alice would be bloody pissed when she found out who he was. Theodore was having too much fun with her, though, to burst the bubble yet. He held the wine bottle over her half-empty glass. "More?"

"Always assume a woman with frozen feet in a Wales rugby jersey five times her size wants more."

He poured wine into her glass. "I'll remember that next time I carry a woman through the snow and have to lend her my favorite item of clothing." He hadn't minded. She'd had a rough night, and he spent so many nights alone in his temporary digs. It was nice to have someone to hang out with. Especially someone who was obviously smart and pretty.

She snuggled her glass to her chest. "I can't believe you have a working fireplace."

The flame's light danced over her dark hair and was reflected in her warm hazel eyes. Keeping his eyes off her was impossible. Mischievous little smiles kept drawing his attention to her mouth.

"I can't believe people don't demand it," he said. "Though,

given I paid nearly five dollars for a piece of wood, I can see why not."

She nodded. "Yeah, DC prices are ridiculous."

They were. But they were that high in the UK, too, only for different items. He couldn't get over what people had to pay for in the US—from copyright protection to healthcare. Paying as much as he had for firewood was merely an additional insult.

Her gaze flicked around his flat, a fully-furnished, also-over-priced piece of real estate to lie his head for the next few months—or however long his recent consulting job took.

Her lips pursed. "Why are you here anyway? And how do you know Edison Tech? What do you do?"

"Ah, the famous question everyone here seems to be super excited about." He'd been there for a full week, and at least five times a day, people had asked him what he did. It was downright crackers that was the first question anyone in this city voiced.

At first, he'd told them "management." Their mouths would open a little, and they'd nod with a long "ah" sound.

Then, when that got boring, he'd changed it up a bit. So far, he'd declared himself a professional mourner, bingo caller, iceberg mover, and—his all-time favorite—a peacock wrangler. None of it was untrue if you thought about it. He often had to deal with tears, lucky draws, icy glares, and preening egos.

However, with what little he knew about Alice, she'd want the reality. "I tell the truth." That was as much as he could tell her, given his non-disclosure agreement for this gig.

She half laughed. "Okay. I get it. People talk about work too much here anyway."

She drained her wine glass, then held it out for more. He obliged.

When a cute little hiccup left her throat, she pressed a finger to her sternum. "I'm going to regret this in the morning. Especially when I have to figure out how to get home, get changed and get to work on time." Her hands flew to her lips. "Oops. Talked about work again."

"Are you between boyfriends?" He couldn't get over how the woman wasn't snatched up already. She was pretty, direct and had to be smart if she worked for Edison Tech.

Her chin jutted back in surprise. "Between?"

"If you had one, he'd have picked you up tonight."

An adorable snort came out of her nose, and she waved her hand. "In DC? I could be married, and he'd have called me a taxi." Though none seemed willing to get her tonight as they'd discovered. Ran through five cab companies, all of whom had laughed as if they'd asked someone to drive her to the moon. Too bad his rental was snowed under as well.

He wasn't too sorry, however. "So, no man in your life. Lucky me. Though it's been Kiss a Ginger Day for over an hour, and I'm not getting very lucky here."

Her face fell, tension gripping her shoulders.

"Just teasing. Not trying to shag you, love. Won't even give you the pleasure of my kiss. Not proper."

"That is so British."

"Okay, then." He slapped his lap. "Jump aboard."

"You'd faint from pure pleasure." She breathed into her wine glass.

He winked. "I give you permission to keep going if I do. Full consent."

A fit of giggles caught her. "I wouldn't want you to feel used."

"I appreciate you protecting my virtue. You're a good woman, Alice."

She pushed at his shoulder. "You're funny. Most guys in this town have no sense of humor. Get ready to be jumped at every turn. Unless you have a girlfriend, of course."

A lightning bolt of anger went through his heart. No girlfriend—at least not anymore. "She's back in Wales." He checked his watch. "She should be catching her flight to Ibiza for her honeymoon any minute." The words burned in his throat.

"Excuse me?"

"Married my best mate." He took a slug of wine. Ex-friend, more like it. And for the life of him, he didn't know why he told her that.

She let her gaze drift to the fire. "That's not very best-matey, if you ask me." Her words were a little loose, like the wine's effects had taken hold.

"Still got them a gift. Made sure it got into their suitcases before they left."

She sliced her eyes his way. "Tell me it was something *deserving*." She leaned over as if her balance was also being compromised.

"A few well-placed spiders in her trousseau. Planted by a friend." He shrugged. "Nothing major." Though incredibly satisfying.

She gasped; though it was through her ear-to-ear grin, showing him she was hardly upset about his incredibly juvenile act. Still wasn't sorry about it.

"So much restraint, Theodore." She mock-punched him in the arm. "I'd have gone for something much bigger. Sheep dung, at least. In fact, you know what?"

She dramatically set down her glass, wine splashing a little on her hand. She licked it off, then leaned over to him. "We're both recent victims of interpersonal crimes, so we must celebrate today's holiday after all." Definitely slurring now. "It's my New Year's Resolution. Take control." She hiccupped and pointed to her forehead. "Keep eyezopen. Gather dataz. Make good choizes. Deztineeeeee."

She squinted at him. "You haz nice eyezzz." She then launched herself at him, and he found not only his arms full of her, but her mouth firmly on his.

In general, he found the act of kissing to be pleasant enough. But when she slipped him a little tongue, slow, soft, and hot, his standards instantly raised. His arms mashed her closer to him. Any thought about how what they were doing was wrong disappeared as soon as the tip of her tongue touched his.

Her weight shifted and—*ffyc*—she straddled his lap.

She came up for air, and brushed her hair off her face. "I don't care if you did make up Kizz a Ginger Day–"

"I didn't." Somehow, he got the words out in a long breath. The day was real, though he'd been teasing about her fulfilling on it.

"Oh, good." She kissed him again, and if anyone asked him, he'd say moving to America could be on the table. She was that good.

She broke the lip hold again. "I'm zzleepy." Her lids were at half-mast. She'd had too much to drink. While his manhood was ready to go forth and conquer, his morals— the spoilsports—took hold. Time to stop.

She leaned forward, put forehead to forehead. "Hey, I got an idea."

"Me, too. Time to sleep, love." He pushed her off his lap, and she dramatically slumped to her side of the couch.

"Awww, come on. *Revenge is ourzz*." She pounded the seat cushion, but let her head fall back.

He rose and pulled a blanket off the rocking chair in the corner. When he turned around, she'd curled into herself against the back of the couch, eyes closed. "I'm very, very good at revenge," she said softly.

He couldn't help but laugh. "I bet you are." After securing the blanket around her form, he turned off the lights. Time for bed himself.

Voicing what happened between him and Beatrice had taken its usual toll. A ball of ice formed in his chest, and he had to shove all the anger and betrayal into that little frozen box he kept close to his heart.

What had been worse than her declaration she'd never loved him was Canton's lack of apology. Just a shrug and "should have stayed home more" thrown at him when Theodore had confronted the guy.

Perhaps he'd told Alice about Beatrice's betrayal because she was easy to talk to. She didn't throw sad puppy eyes at him like so many people had those first two months.

That would only make tomorrow morning harder. She might never speak to him again after she was re-introduced to him at Edison Tech's staff meeting, a mere ten hours from then.

The company wasn't doing well, and the owners wanted him to uncover what was happening. He was sworn to secrecy, unable to talk about why he was brought in, just that as a management consultant, he was there to, ostensibly, "reduce all redundancies."

Her name was on the suspect list. And when she found out? He could only hope she kidded about her payback skills.

3

———

Alice leaned into her desk and squinted at the computer screen. Something was not right on her boss's expense report. Roger spent two hundred dollars on lunch? Then again, DC prices.

Patty knocked on her door frame. "Still can't believe Roger made us come in today."

"I can." The man was a drill sergeant. And a prick, something she'd voice to him at the appropriate time.

Patty perched herself on the corner of Alice's desk. "What's with the jumper cables?" She pointed at the things taking up far too much space.

"Harrison from marketing returned them. Finally bought his own, which is good because I'm tired of giving him a jump." Tired of car issues altogether.

She discovered that morning hers must have been towed from its spot overnight. She'd go back at lunchtime to retrieve it from the lot. At least DC had a phone number on the signs calling the street a *Snow Emergency Route.*

Also on the day's docket was not dwelling on the cascade of unfortunate events of last night. Or thinking about how she'd spectacularly broken her resolution to make better choices hours into it.

She'd woken up that morning on a stranger's couch under a tartan blanket with a pounding headache. It took a solid minute to remember how the hell she'd gotten there. Far less time to hightail it out once she remembered the Kiss a Ginger guy. *Theodore.* He at least had plugged her phone into a charger near the sofa where she'd passed out. And thank God she was able to get a cab, get home, and get changed for work. It was a miracle she was only an hour late to the office.

Alice pointed at her computer. "Hey, you ever been to the Palm?"

"The restaurant?" Patty fiddled with a pen, stuck it in her bun. "Yeah. Pompous and overpriced."

Roger's weekly expense report might be right, then.

Patty leaned down closer and dropped her voice to a whisper. "Did you get a load of the Jamie Fraser who walked in this morning?"

Patty had three categories for men when she was interested in them. Dark-haired men were Henry Cavills, blonds were Daniel Craigs— "the young one"—and redheads were naturally Sam Heughans. Patty was obsessed with the Jamie Fraser character, in particular. "The rarest unicorn of them all," she'd sighed dramatically over margaritas one night at her most favorite rugby bar.

Alice spun her chair around. "Thought you were going to make babies with the Henry Cavill in the C-suite?" Jerry Maxwell, the vice president of the manufacturing division, was cute with great hair—and he knew it, given he couldn't pass a mirror without pausing to admire himself.

"Not since I found out he still lives with his mother because he's worried about their eighteen parrots. How they might miss him. Apparently, parrots bond with their humans. I'm betting this new Jamie doesn't have parrots."

Her eyes grew distant. "He looks more like he'd have Scottish terriers."

Patty's imagination was vast—and resembled a romance novel.

Alice blew a stray strand of hair out of her face. "I made it a point to not see *anyone* this morning." Thank God for dry shampoo, but second-day hair was always a static nightmare.

Patty pushed off the desk. "Well, how do I look? Good enough for the new Jamie?" She ran her hands down her pencil skirt, then adjusted her sparkly, blue-framed glasses.

"Very sexy librarian. He'd be lucky as sin to nail you behind the historical romance section." She grabbed her portfolio and a pen. "Come on. Monday staff meeting starts in two."

"Still can't believe Roger's making us do this today. I want the chair next to the back, the one with not-heinous lighting."

When they entered the conference room, six other Edison Tech employees were seated around the large walnut table, including Tricia and Stephanie, who threw her yet another pitying glance. Great, they honestly thought she was heartbroken over Roger and not being chosen as Miss December. As far as she cared, Roger could have a woman for every month, national holiday, and even the made-up ones like National Bobblehead Day.

"Good morning, team. Glad to see you made it in, despite a few snowflakes," Roger greeted as he rushed through the glass doors.

A few? Roger should hand out medals for those who showed up.

Clapping his hands together, he rubbed them as if kindling firewood and stood at the head of the table. "I realize it's Friday, but it's time to talk about this new year."

"Let's not," Harrison mumbled as he scrambled to take the

vacant chair next to Alice. On her other side was Patty, sitting under a half-dimmed ceiling light. Alice really needed to call maintenance about the bulb. It could go out anytime.

Roger beamed at everyone. He was entirely too happy that morning. Probably because he'd identified Miss January already. The way a petite blonde, new to the management team, gazed up at him, Alice would bet her life savings he had.

Roger leaned down, knuckles on the table. "A new year means new beginnings. I'm not going to beat around the bushel here. We're starting with assessing the team. Edison hired a management firm to conduct a thorough evaluation of performance, redundancy, and inefficiencies."

A visible groan filled the room, and Roger's smile thinned. "Now, now. I know what you're thinking. You are all valuable, and this is merely to ensure everyone is giving their best work, headed to their best future for themselves and this company." He knocked on the table once.

Harrison leaned over. "He means protecting his future bonuses."

Alice gave him a grimace in solidarity.

Roger clapped his hands together again. "We're starting from the rump up."

Alice stifled a laugh. No one else held back, though. Snickers filled the room. Roger was constantly mixing up words and getting metaphors wrong, like bushel versus bush and rump versus bottom.

"I know whose rump I'd like to start with," Harrison whispered as he eyed Patty. He was fully bald in a sexy rock kind of way and quite handsome. But Patty had a real thing for hair.

Roger theatrically swept his arm toward the conference room door. "Everyone, I'd like to introduce you to Theodore Gaston."

Blood pounded in Alice's ears, her neck, her head. *No way.* The red-headed guy from last night's surprise snow-mageddon walked through the door in a charcoal gray suit and blue tie.

Patty sat up straighter. But if Alice could have faded into the upholstery of her chair, she'd have done it. A crushing flood of memories swamped her. She'd *kissed* the guy last night.

Roger held out a hand to Theodore to shake. "Good to see you again." He turned to the staff. "Many of you met him last night, but given it was my birthday …"

Jesus, keep reminding us already.

"… I told him to stick to just getting to know you. No work talk."

Theodore wrested his hand free, nodded once, then scanned the room. Alice did her level best to hide behind Patty, but because her friend was thin as a pencil, Theodore easily caught her gaze.

One side of his mouth lifted. The man was amused? A buzzing began in Alice's low belly and snaked its way up her spine. So, that was what shame felt like.

She dipped her chin and assessed her manicure.

"Thank you, Mr. Rubenstein. Good day, Edison Tech," he said in a far deeper voice than she recalled.

And *Mr.* Rubenstein? No one called Roger that.

A chorus of "Hi" and "Hello" sounded, mostly female. She risked a glance up. He still stared at her.

"As Mr. Rubenstein stated, I'm Theodore Gaston. And I want to start out by saying, I know I'm not your favorite person already."

A few titters sounded.

Theodore began to walk around the conference table. "Mr. Rubenstein thought it best to keep everyone out of the loop until it was time."

Oh, they'd been out of the loop all right. Though last night, she'd almost been very, very much *in the loop*—the nude one.

"I'm not here to make your life miserable." He stopped and stared at her once more. "I'm here to make it better."

A few of the sales guys visibly shifted, uncomfortable. They were always the first to get put on the chopping block.

Theodore resumed his walk. "Now, I'd like to set up appointments with each of you. A deeper, get-to-know-you meeting. Learn about your relevant and important skills. No preparation needed."

Three hands went up. All female again. *Shocker.* Because Alice was woman enough to admit Theodore was a hottie with those bluer-than-blue eyes and a frame that could carry a woman around in the snow without breaking a sweat.

He didn't look like he only got five hours of sleep and drank too much. Oh, crap. She did, didn't she? She hadn't even put on make-up that morning, thinking it'd be an ordinary day of her computer screen seeing more of her than anything or anyone else.

Why should she care what Theodore thought? Maybe because her entire future was at stake.

She'd heard rumors the higher-ups weren't happy with how things were going. Sales were down. Marketing costs were up. She never thought they'd bring someone in to assess the entire staff, however. They should be assessing Roger. He was the one who dictated everything down to when the plants were watered.

Theodore pointed at Tricia, whose hand nearly touched the ceiling. "Yes, Miss …"

"Brown. Tricia Brown from HR." The woman beamed at him. "It was good to meet you last night, Mr. Gaston. Given I work in HR, perhaps I could help you navigate the team?"

By how she eyed him, she'd like to navigate him all right. Straight into those very expensive-looking trousers.

"Please, call me Theodore." He'd almost circled to her side of the table now. "We're going to do the interviews randomly. I think starting with …"

He looked over to her, which sent highly inappropriate tingles down her body.

He moved to where she sat. "Miss Crawford? You're in accounting, correct?"

"Correct. And it's Alice." She did not smile. "As you know."

"Alice. I heard you had a bit of car trouble last night. Everything sorted?" he asked in that melodic British accent. His blue eyes sparkled. He was enjoying himself.

"Sorted," she said sharply. In her periphery, she could see all eyes were on them.

"Good."

Everyone's phones pinged and vibrated in the room.

"Right on time," he said. "Meeting requests should have landed in your inbox."

Everyone, including Alice, lifted their phones to see a calendar request showing their time slot with Theodore. *Chit-Chat with Theodore*, it read. How very friendly—and ridiculous.

Alice quickly glanced around to gauge reactions. Tricia's mouth twisted, clearly unhappy with her time slot.

Harrison waved his phone. "And if we have a conflict? Have to move it?"

Roger held up his hand. "There is no greater priority than this."

Theodore had finally moved his body, his scent drifting away from her. He made his way to the head of the table. "No, no. If you have an emergency or really need to change your time, just let me know."

Roger's face fell, his eyes darkening a little. She recognized that look. Countering the guy who's writing his management fee checks? Not very smart. Then again, catering to Roger's ego hadn't gotten her very far at Edison.

Theodore didn't seem to notice he'd semi-insulted Roger. Just stood there in his beautifully cut suit, smiling, basking in the gaze of every person around the table. He enjoyed the attention. She didn't recall him being arrogant last night. He was fun—and dishonest with her. Time to remind him he should tread carefully in case he got any notions of yielding power over her. What he'd done the night before had to have broken some ethical rules somewhere.

She cleared her throat and raised her hand.

Theodore pointed at her. "Oh, no need to do that. Ask away."

"Mr. Gaston—"

"Just Theodore is fine."

The women gave each other sidelong glances, like secret messages being handed back and forth in seventh grade. Every single one of them was already into him. By the look of confidence on his face, he was quite comfortable with being admired.

Alice laid a hand delicately on her breastbone. "Don't you mean Theodore Gaston the *Fourth*?"

Patty gasped a little. "Is he famous or something?" she whispered out of the side of her mouth. "Dibs on him."

A lazy smile broke out on his face. "So my mum and dad say. You have a question?"

Alice laid her phone face down on the table. "I can't make it at eleven." Or ever.

"No problem. We'll talk right after this meeting."

God, she hated her life.

Roger beamed at her. "Excellent. Now, meeting adjourned. Have a …"

She didn't hear the rest of his words. She was out of her chair like a shot and leaving the conference room from the back exit. She hightailed it to her office and closed the door.

Think. Think. Think.

She was a professional, and her job at Edison was important to her. She was pretty sure, however, straddling the new management consultant's balls, as she'd done last night, wouldn't be viewed as a *relevant and important* skill. If it were, she'd have fired herself.

A knock on her door sounded. She didn't need to open the door to know it was him—the guy whose hands held her future.

A muffled male voice chuckled on the other side of the door. "Didn't take you for someone who ran away."

As if he knew anything about her. She yanked the door open. "You have some nerve ..."

He advanced on her, and she had no choice but to retreat. He closed the door behind him.

No words came to her mind. It was because he was too close. He smelled good. Like he'd put on cologne, which was not something she normally thought about with men.

"About last night," he said.

She crossed her arms. "It was highly unethical of you."

"Me?"

"Luring me to your place. Kissing me."

"It was Kiss a Ginger Day." He dipped his chin, his tone as serious as if delivering critical news. "And for the record, you jumped me."

She gasped, dropped her arms. "I did not."

"Oh, yes, you did. Climbed right aboard." He pointed to his crotch. "Straddled my goods. In fact, I feel incredibly used." He batted his eyelashes up at the ceiling.

Crap. More fuzzy memories swam up to the surface where *she* was the one to launch herself at him last night. She wanted to smack that smirk off his face. She settled for slapping his pec. Oh, hard muscle. She quickly brought her hand back and clasped it to her belly. "I could get you fired."

He chuckled. "Maybe. Then again, I did help you find your car."

"Ah, but you didn't help me push it out." Jamie Frasier would have.

"And mess up my chances to spend more time with you? Not on your life."

"You think you had a chance? Not on *your* life." As if she'd be interested in him after hiding who he really was.

She circled to the safety of her desk, putting it between Theodore and herself. "You should have told me last night you were an Edison consultant." In fact, *Roger* should have told her. Then again, when had he ever been upfront with her about anything.

He shoved his hands into his pockets. "I didn't lie to you."

"You didn't tell the truth either." A realization hit her. "You were spying last night."

"I was an observer. You can tell a lot about how happy people are by watching their social interactions." His gaze raked over her. "You were quite friendly."

She pointed at him. "See? Unethical." If he thought he could blackmail her because they'd had an *interaction*, he could shove a bobblehead up his ass.

"That's not what I meant. I mean, you *were* friendly ... before ..." He scrubbed his hair. "Listen. I enjoyed getting to know you. Nothing ultimately happened, and—"

"And that's the way it's staying." She sharply nodded her chin. *Period. End of statement.* "We're strictly business. I'm very serious about my job."

He rocked back on his heels and peered down at her with those sparkly blue eyes. "Good." He kept studying her.

"What?"

"You're especially pretty when annoyed."

Did he have any boundaries? "Go charm one of your admirers out there." She waved her fingers toward her door and the hallway beyond.

"Admirers? I've been in the building for less than an hour. But I see what's happening here."

Nothing was *happening* here. "Oh, really?" A sudden roil went off in her stomach. She clutched her belly as if that would quell the queasy feeling.

"Playing hard to get." He tapped a finger on his lips. "I like it. A woman like you should."

"Theodore," she said slowly, putting her palms together.

He leaned closer, bringing his woodsy scent closer to her. "Alice."

She blinked. She forgot what she was going to say. It was because she was hungover and sleep-deprived; that was all.

"Did you get your car unstuck?" he asked. "I didn't see it this morning on Porter."

"You live on Ordway."

He shrugged one shoulder. "I checked on it."

"Oh. That was nice of you. It's been towed." Which was yet another problem she would have to solve. "I'll get it later."

"You came to work instead? Dedicated."

"And stupid." She should have worked from home, avoided that little run-in altogether. But when had she ever taken a day off?

His face grew serious. "There's nothing about you that's stupid."

"Oh?" She arched her eyebrows at him. "Last night? That was—"

"Highlight of my life."

She crossed her arms, refusing to be further charmed by him. "Then you need to get a better life." Her hands slapped to her sides. "Is this part of the interview? Talking like this about goods straddling and my car?"

He peered around her desk at her feet. "You going to retrieve it in those heels? Shame to kill another pair."

"Maybe. Yes. I don't know." Her head was pounding anew, and she rubbed one temple. Enough of that. "I need coffee."

She rounded her desk and yanked open her door. Tricia and Stephanie jerked upright. Patty stood behind them, arms crossed, her foot tapping, clearly disapproving of the eavesdroppers. Patty always had Alice's back.

Stephanie giggled, and Tricia adopted her disapproving frown. "We were seeing if Alice was free for lunch," Steph said.

"Sadly not," Theodore answered for her. "We have our first interview. Over lunch."

What the...?

"Ooo, a date," Patty whispered and slowly nodded.

Roger came up behind them. "Ladies. Call a meeting or something?" He hated it when the women gathered, probably because he didn't want any of them to compare notes on him.

Tricia slowly turned toward him, her lips curling into a cunning smile. "Seems Alice and Theodore are having a date."

Alice almost corrected her, because no way was she going on a date with Kiss a Ginger guy. But then Roger stepped closer, disdain coloring his face. "Oh? Is that appropriate?"

Nothing about the last twenty-four hours had been appropriate. But even if Roger was her boss, she'd be damned if she'd think he could pull that stunt. According to Tricia, the guy dated half the office in addition to withholding information about his real plans for replacing the CFO. If anyone was wrong, it was him.

You know what? It would help to have a guy with her if

she had to go to a place where they towed cars. They weren't usually in the safest areas of DC. She could pretend they were going out for lunch and do that instead. It would be Theodore's penance for putting her in that position.

She swiveled her head to gaze at him. "You ever been to the Palm? I hear it's a great place for a job-related lunch for that interview." She then looked right at Roger, who flushed red with anger. "Since it's such a priority and all."

It was ridiculously early for lunch, but the whole scenario needed handling—immediately. After she got her car, of course. Then she'd have a serious talk with Theodore about boundaries. Good plan all around.

"No, I haven't," Theodore said. "Lead the way." He gestured for her to bypass the crowd.

She snatched up her purse and her scarf and marched straight to the elevator. She wasn't feeling great so maybe a little food would help.

The door opened immediately. She stepped inside and leaned against the railing, feeling a little dizzy. Theodore followed her inside, and the doors shut them inside together —and alone.

He immediately stepped closer, bringing his scent into her space again. "You sure you want to go to the Palm?"

His eyes really were otherworldly blue, and he truly smelled amazing. Like cinnamon and leather.

"No, I don't, I'd like to ..." Her words were stopped because his arm circled her waist and yanked her flush to him. Oh, strong. Her head felt like it was floating off her body. He brought his face closer to hers. He had such nice lips.

"I do, huh?"

She said that aloud? She sucked in a breath, the elevator walls waving in her sight. Dots appeared in her vision; her knees buckled. Then ...

4

———————

Theodore stood before Alice's larder and sighed. "Bloody hell, what you Americans try to pass off as tea is a crime."

"I suppose you found the tea bags?" Her voice was strained. "I don't need any."

He peeked through her kitchen archway to where she lay on the couch, ice pack held to her forehead. "No one needs these." She needed a proper tea kettle with some loose-leaf tea. Chamomile to calm her easily rattled nerves.

He strode over to the trash bin, stepped on the pedal, and when the lid lifted, dropped the no-name generic box into the bin. "There. In their proper place." A coffee shop that served better tea had to be around the corner. They were around *every* corner in DC.

The ice pack crinkled in the living room. Poor girl collapsed just as the elevator doors opened, and half a dozen people tried to rush in. He'd half carried her out like a limp rag doll. Not a single person asked about it. Bloody cold, if you asked him.

She'd finally emerged from her fainting spell in the lobby as he carried her in his arms. She'd wiggled so hard, trying to get free, they had to have resembled two fish in some weird mating dance.

Convincing her to get into the rideshare car so he could escort her home wasn't any easier, either.

Still, once inside, she'd plopped down on her couch, not bothering to shed her shoes or coat. She had to be suffering.

He leaned against the archway and stared down at her. Even under present conditions, she was still quite pretty—though stubborn. "You get bad headaches like this a lot?"

"Only when I drink too much, get no sleep, and crumple in front of men who hold my future in their hands."

That last part wasn't exactly true. Even if his assessment found she was lacking somehow—and that was growing more doubtful by the second—it wasn't a guarantee she'd be sacked. He was there to tell the truth, as he'd said. And his brief stint that morning at Edison Tech revealed she was a committed worker. Any personal interest he had in Alice had nothing to do with his work at Edison—or hers. Besides, he wasn't much of a man if he didn't make sure she was okay after crumpling before him in the elevator.

He sighed, pushed off the door jamb, and grabbed a bottle of water from a large pack sitting on the counter. "I'd never use my position to harm your future. Now, take the day off. We have your car to retrieve. Call in sick."

Finally, the ice bag was lifted from her forehead as she looked at him, aghast. "That's not very management consultant of you. Aren't you here to get us to work more?"

He winked. "Smarter, not harder, love."

"I've always hated that saying. It hides a multitude of sins, like delegating to everyone but yourself."

She was most definitely a smart one. "What patronizing, cliched saying do you think would work at Edison?"

"Ah, so the interview has begun." She let the ice pack fall

to the floor, then reached over to rummage in her purse. She pulled out a bottle of Tylenol.

He moved to where she lay prone on the couch, a blanket over her legs. He handed her the bottle of water. "Afraid, given the sad state of your larder, this is all you're getting."

She popped open the Tylenol bottle. "Thanks, and you can go, really. You have work to do, and so do I. I won't be any more trouble to you."

"What?" He slapped his chest. "And miss a chance to celebrate Inconvenience Yourself Day?" He gestured for her to make room for him, and she bent her knees. He parked himself on the opposite end of the couch.

She lightly tapped him with her foot. "You're making these days up." She threw back two pills and took a long swig of water.

Ah, cynical, too. "Google it."

She snuggled back down against her ice pack. "Later. Okay, if you insist on helping. First, I need just a few minutes, then—" she lowered the ice "—you can help me get my car. Consider it payback for your—"

"Irresistibility?"

"Not telling me who you were last night. Then, afterward, I'm going back to Edison. I have a ton of work to do."

He crossed his arms. "What do you think of the company?"

She pointed at him. "Oh, no. We will be doing this in the office. Nowhere else. We've already crossed a million lines."

"Well, technically, you did the crossing—"

"What?" She sat up and punched his arm.

"Ow." He rubbed his bicep, not that it hurt him. "Still trying to cop a feel, I see."

"You're unconscionable, you know that?"

If she only knew the thoughts in his mind—being this close to her again. But he shouldn't voice them. "Ah, not today. It's Be Humble Day. Why do you want to go back to work so badly?"

Her phone buzzed on the coffee table. She pointed at it. "Because *that* will happen all day if I don't get back." She lifted her phone and peered at the screen.

"One of the main delegators?"

"It's Roger trying to call. Probably wanting to make sure I wasn't trashing him over crab cakes at the Palm with you." She slapped a hand over her mouth. "I shouldn't have said that."

"Don't like your boss?"

"He's … fine." She kicked off the blanket and tried to rise but fell back down.

His hand landed on her back, just to steady her, of course. "Tell him you're taking the day off," he said. "Unless fainting is an everyday occurrence for you. Plus, there's the matter of your car."

"I don't take days off."

"Not even for International Accounting Day? November 10."

"Not even then." She swung her gaze to him. "Why are you so obsessed with these days, anyway?"

He shrugged and laid back a little more. "My question is, why aren't more people? The chance to go 'round today and say things like 'Happy Supermarket Employee Day' and 'Happy Pink Shirt Day'—only that's in Canada today."

She eyed him. "I think it's because you enjoy disarming people."

"Who me? I'd never. Especially not today. It's Scout's Founder's Day. Chance for all Scouts and Guides to reaffirm their oaths of duty, service, and truth and contemplate how such values are still relevant in today's world." He nodded his chin sharply.

"Oh, Theodore." She let her head fall back. "You're at least funny."

Her phone buzzed again. She brought it to her face, then let it fall to the seat cushion.

"Let me guess," he said. "Roger wanting you back at the office."

"Maybe." She swiveled her head to find Theodore still smiling at her. "Ready to take me to my car?"

"I'd love nothing more." He rose. "Come on, then."

She texted a quick message and held it up to his face so he could read it.

<<Not feeling well. Taking a sick day if that's okay.>>

"Happy?" she asked.

He held out his hand. "Not in the slightest. You shouldn't have to beg to take care of yourself."

As he pulled her up to standing, she wobbled. He reached out to help her, and she immediately melted into him. His arms went around her. That time, she didn't push off or try to do the wiggle fish dance. For several long seconds, they stood there, wrapped in a semi-hug. It was nice.

"If you really have the bubonic plague, and you give it to me, and I die," he said. "I will haunt you forever. Especially on National Accountant's Day."

Her body shook with laughter. He didn't let go of her, though he wouldn't be surprised if she shoved him off. As she'd pointed out—repeatedly—they were work colleagues. Technically, he was a consultant. She was an employee of Edison Tech. But he was supposed to evaluate her performance, right? See who was the source of trouble at Edison? Because there most definitively was a problem there. He already knew it wasn't because of her.

"You really do smell good." Her words were muffled into his shirt.

So did she. "Flowers. Jasmine. That's what you smell like to me."

Her body rumbled against his chest when she murmured and went straight through his shirt to parts of his body that were most definitely inappropriate. He hardened almost instantly.

She lifted her head up to gaze at him. "I don't know what's gotten into me today."

"You're overcome with lust and longing for me."

She threw him a skeptical look. "You have it backward. You're finding it impossible to be separated from my magnetic charm and ability to wrestle numbers into submission."

His hands moved to cup her face. "Yes, impossible."

They stood there, staring at one another for a beat.

She broke first. "We can't."

"Can't what?"

She was back to clutching her fingers. "This chemistry thing."

"Ah, so it wasn't just the wine you consumed last night." She felt their pull to one another, too.

"It might have been why we …" She twirled her hands in the air as if he could read them like sign language.

"We haven't done anything. Yet."

She grasped her bottom lip between her teeth. "See? That … *yet* thing is a problem. We don't have enough information about each other and it feels risky, working together to—"

"It doesn't have to be a problem. What if we merely delay?" The Edison Tech job was only a few months long— shorter if he could get to the bottom of what was happening with the company quickly.

"A delay," she repeated, her mouth deliciously close to his.

"Which." He cocked his head back and forth. "Actually may be an issue now that I think about it. I mean, the way you kiss ..." He glanced once more down at her lips. He didn't often feel that automatic pull toward someone.

"It was Kiss a Ginger Day," she whispered.

His chin jutted back. "Broke out the special ones for me last night, did you?"

Her dark eyes were fixed on him, and the need to work over her mouth with his arose so hard he found himself almost advancing on her. "You know, to even things out, perhaps I should be the one to kiss you next," he said. "That way, it neutralizes the line crossing you believe we did. Cancels it out."

"Oh, good point. That way, it would be like it never happened."

Was she kidding? There was no way he could think it never happened. But waiting to act on their desires couldn't be that hard. They were grown-ups, for God's sake.

She turned, her eyes glazing as if in thought. "Hmm. I suppose it would be a good data point." She lifted her gaze to him. "See if we're any good at it without wine."

"And if we are—"

She held up a hand. "We'd need to know a lot more about each other for anything else." The way her eyes skimmed over his body told him everything. She was interested, which made his ego swell and his logic go on holiday.

"Tell you what," he said. "When this project is over, if you still want my bod, I'll meet you at the bobblehead store on National Bobblehead Day."

"There's a store?"

"Yes, in London."

"Pick a day that's closer than January of next year, and I'll consider it ."

And didn't that light up his ego. "Can't wait, can you?"

She crossed her arms. "Test me."

Smart woman, keeping the ball in her court. He rather

liked the challenge. When was the last time he ever waited that long to exercise his interest. Perhaps it could work. See how long they could last?

"Okay," he said. "I'll pick a day. But the deal is you must keep your hands north of my privates until then." Otherwise, one touch from her, and who knew where they'd end up. He pointed at her. "As hard as it's going to be. Right, then. Our freedom day will be National BAE Day."

"When's that?"

"June 10."

"That *would* give us a good amount of time." She nodded her head sharply. "All right, until then, your hands are not allowed near me. Especially not …" She circled her breasts.

"Your breasts?"

She nibbled on her lip. "They'd be hard to resist. I mean it."

They were all he could stare at now. Imagining how soft her skin might be, the color of her nipples. "You like your"— he dipped his chin to her chest—"assets to be well appreciated?"

"They're high-value assets. They deserve special treatment."

He closed the distance between them. "Everything about you should get special treatment."

She cocked her head. "Who *are* you?"

"Theodore Gaston the Fourth. Again, at your service. Now, about that kiss. To neutralize."

"One." She stepped forward, tapping her cheek for him to peck it.

"You have *got* to be kidding." He scrubbed a finger over his bottom lip. "First, you give me the kiss of a lifetime on what really should be an international holiday. Then, you only allow me a grandma peck? My lips are insulted to be so rejected."

"Okay. One on the lips. Then we'll see if it was the wine or something else."

He immediately yanked her closer to him, her breasts mashing against his chest. "Then it's countdown to National BAE Day." He silenced any more words with his mouth as he tangled his tongue with hers. Breathing in her flowery scent through his nose, he felt her hands slide up his chest to around his neck. When her hands curled into his hair, he deepened his kiss.

He spun her, lips still connected, until her back hit her front door. She murmured into his mouth, which hardened him further.

Her leg rose up his calf and circled around him. Bending his knees, he lifted her slightly, so he fit more snugly between her legs. *Ffyc*, his cock ached. He continued to explore her mouth, grinding against her. He could do that for an hour. The kissing part, that was. The rest of him would blow in under three minutes at the rate they were going.

When they finally broke, both panting, his lips stinging, her eyes brighter, he lowered her to her feet.

"Well neutralized," she panted.

He sucked in a long breath. "Yeah. Uh, not at all."

"I know, right?" She licked her bottom lip. "It's real. We should go before—"

"Good idea." Otherwise, he'd have her back on the couch where all limits would be shattered.

He stepped backward, straightening his suit coat. "Though I may have to hobble to my car."

She smiled up at him. "Good." She spun to crack open the door and nearly collided with Roger. What the devil? He almost didn't believe his own eyes. A CEO of a place in as much trouble as Edison shouldn't be standing in Alice's hallway. Certainly not in the middle of the day.

"Roger," she said brightly.

"Thought I heard moaning. You that sick?" He glanced up, finally catching Theodore behind her. The cheapskate held a bouquet of grocery store flowers with the price sticker emblazoned on the plastic wrapping. The man was wearing a Rolex, for Christ's sake. "Theodore," he spat. "What the hell are you doing here?"

"I'd ask the same of you." He crossed his arms. "Always check in on employees when they're off?"

The man widened his stance, rolled his shoulders. "Only the ones I'm involved with."

5

———

Roger and Theodore glared at one another like two bighorn sheep about to headbutt. Great. She had a car to retrieve, and men's egos would have to take a backseat. Especially when one of the big rams had just declared he and Alice were involved—what a crock—and the other had just kissed her lips until they were bruised.

She carefully took the outstretched flowers. "Thank you for these." Though now she wondered how the hell he got there so fast. She'd texted him less than ten minutes ago.

"Are you okay, Alice?" Roger looked genuinely concerned. "I heard what happened. I was out at a meeting and came right over."

Who the hell told him? "Um, Theodore graciously drove me home. I wasn't feeling well. But he's about to leave, and I need to go get my car. Then I'll be back in the office." Her voice had that fake lilt she hated.

Technically, all of that was true. She left out the part where Theodore was going with her to the impound lot.

She turned to Theodore. "You were about to call a rideshare, right?"

"Yes. Right," Theodore said without taking his eyes off Roger.

Roger's chin lifted. "You can go back with me, Theodore."

Theodore bristled. "I have a few errands to run. See you back at Edison." He strode to the door and disappeared through it. So much for his help in getting her car.

His sudden disappearance, however, gave her an opportunity to clear things up with her boss. "Listen, Roger." She turned to him. "About last night."

"You left in a hurry."

"I heard you're about to advertise the CFO position. I thought that was what our last few dinners were about." She had to ask him—straight away. "Is that what *you* thought they were about?"

"I have to advertise the role. It's all part of the process."

That was his answer? "And our dinner meetings? You told Theodore we were involved."

He sniffed. "That was to give you an out with him if you needed it."

The way his right eye twitched told her he was lying. "Theodore gave me a ride. That's all."

"Besides, you're clearly only interested in business, so ..." He shrugged. "Wasn't going to work out."

Oh, my God. He thought they *could* have been dates? "And about being considered for CFO—"

"At the right time."

"When is the right time? Brian left months ago, and I have ideas on how we can improve some things. Remember when I brought up—"

He raised his hand, halting her speech. "Listen, you're good at what you do. Very good."

"But?"

"But don't get ahead of your skis."

Hard to do when she didn't ski at all. "Not sure I understand how I'm doing that. You said I was all business, which I'd think you'd want."

"It's all good, Alice." He laid his hands on her shoulders, and she suppressed a shudder. "Now, don't work too hard this weekend. But I do need those reports on my desk first thing Monday." He pointed at her, and then he strode out.

She'd been dismissed—but as a CFO candidate or a potential date? The thought of Roger touching her made her skin crawl. She needed him to see her as promotion-worthy, not romantic material.

And why was he so sure she'd dedicate her free time to Edison if he wasn't promising her anything in return?

Anger rose hard and fast. She often worked weekends; she thought she was showing her dedication to the company. Shit. He was never giving her that promotion, was he? No way would she go into the office now.

She'd get her car *herself*, then maybe do something completely frivolous and decadent. Go to a spa. Redecorate her apartment. *Take up skiing.*

She called the 800 number she'd jotted down from the street sign that morning. Once she found out where her car was, she grabbed her purse, locked up, and rounded the corner only to run straight into a hard body. She screeched just as a loud male voice yelled.

"Theodore!" She slapped his chest. "You scared the shit out of me."

"You can't stop attacking me, can you?" He looked over his shoulder. "Roger gone?"

"Yes, why aren't you?"

"I promised to take you to get your car. I only left so Roger wouldn't get the wrong idea. Speaking of which, why didn't Roger offer since—?"

"Because he's … busy," she quickly lied. She'd rather have said because he was a prick. It wouldn't have been the smartest thing to say to a consultant evaluating your performance. Perhaps Theodore valued undying loyalty—even if she was beginning to see her allegiance to Edison wasn't advancing her career as she'd hoped.

Theodore's blue eyes stay fixed on hers. "And?"

"Nothing. Let's go."

Thankfully, Theodore didn't question her about Roger's declaration of being involved with her on the way over to Galin and Son's impound lot. She could only handle one crisis at a time.

The lot was as she'd expected. Cars parked haphazardly inside a fenced-in yard. Chain link fencing standing at least twenty feet high to keep anyone out. Dirty slush everywhere from last night's snow, albeit melting at a good clip in the harsh sun that had broken through the clouds.

"Note to self. Don't ever leave my car alone again," she muttered to Theodore.

A man in a flannel shirt and down jacket, a cigarette dangling out of one side of his mouth, gruffly puffed out, "That'll be $675. Cash. ATM is over there." He jerked his head to a gray and black ATM machine wrapped in thick chains that stood to the side of the booth.

"How convenient," Theodore sniffed.

"Yeah," the guy's face split into a grin. "She's lucky. The northwest lot ain't got one." He appeared quite proud of his little machine. Alice pushed her card in and began to tap the dirty screen. She would have to hose herself down after their field trip.

"She's so lucky," Theodore agreed. "I mean, stranded during a snowstorm, car unable to move, no one else out and about. But just in case her car was in the way of, oh, I don't know, a snowmobile that needed to park or Santa's sleigh, you guys come along and liberate the spot no one in the city needed all for the bargain price of $675. You must be very proud of the work you do."

What was he doing? "Um, Theodore, let's just go." She slid the money across to the lot attendant.

His beefy hand immediately snatched it up. "The parking rules are the parking rules, Your Royal Highness." The guy grinned at him, then turned away to watch whatever he was watching on his tiny TV screen.

It took them a full twenty minutes to find her car, and her shoes were likely ruined from the dirty slush, but they didn't look any worse for the wear. She cracked open the driver's side. "Remind me to stay home when it snows again."

"Still can't get over that he asked for almost seven hundred dollars with a straight face. Whatever happened to fair warning where they merely leave a ticket on your windshield, adorned with a smiley face?" Theodore climbed into the passenger side.

The man had quite the optimistic streak. "Clearly, you've not parked on a snow emergency route. The snowplows take precedence."

"No chivalry in that."

Theodore was hung up on that notion for sure. Not that it was a bad thing. For instance, he hadn't asked about Roger. She'd still have to bring it up. They needed to handle the gossip her boss—or anyone else—might have started back at the office. A few people there, like Tricia, were motormouths.

She clutched the steering wheel with both hands, faced forward, and tried to forget the fact that she was once again trapped inside a car with Theodore's scent. He smelled like a man—wool and cinnamon and something else she couldn't name but really, really wanted to. Even Theodore's weird obsession with made-up holidays couldn't dampen the odd pull she had toward him.

She would have gotten buck naked with him in a second if they hadn't been interrupted. And that wasn't something she did often and certainly *never* with someone she didn't know.

Get a grip, Alice. And keep it, she told herself. Their attraction had to be some strange concoction of pheromones. Something scientific, easily explained.

As soon as she pulled out of the lot, Theodore glanced around. "Let's have lunch. I could eat a horse. Fair warning, too, we're going to talk business. Have our interview, starting with why Roger showed up at your apartment."

Oh, shit. He would force the issue after all. "I have no idea. We had a few dinners together. It was nothing. It was to talk about work, but some people have an idea he thinks it might have been more. But my job performance should not be evaluated on his delusions." Or his decision to not promote her. *Prick. Prick. Prick.*

"If he's ever taken advantage of his position—"

"No. Pure consent to talk business over wine and salmon. But ancient history." She tittered a little. "Meant nothing. All is well. It's over. Like a minor blip. Like … nothing." Gah, she was rambling when she needed him to think she was professional, C-suite material.

And now that she'd learned Roger didn't believe in her, a burning desire to prove him wrong grew like a rising sun. Perhaps Theodore could help. If he gave her a glowing review, maybe Roger would rethink his hesitation around her promotion.

"Okay," he sighed. "You don't strike me as someone who gets easily bowled over, so I accept your answer."

"How noble."

He looked over at her, brow furrowed. "Whatever you tell me, I'll believe."

His tone was so sincere, she believed him. "Good." It was

time to get down to business. "So, what's our story going to be?"

"Story?"

"The one we need to tell Patty when we get back after us supposedly having a lunch interview. The one we're going to make up about us because people clearly saw us leave and Roger found you in my apartment." She was so over being considered gossip-worthy—and he'd gotten her into that mess by catching her when she fainted, which had likely started a snowball of rumors. A tad unfair, but she was sticking with it. "People might assume we were … you know …"

"Shagging?"

He nailed it. "Patty can start the counter gossip immediately. We have to neutralize this thing." She might be mad at her boss, but she wouldn't let her whole life at Edison fall apart. It was time to make good on that New Year's resolution.

He stared at her, blinking.

"What?" she asked. "This is important. We need some believable details."

He faced the windshield again. "I was magnificent. The best you ever had. I've ruined you for all other men."

She choked out a laugh. He was impossible. "You have it backward. I am now the benchmark for which you assess all other women. I own your body and soul. Bella Hadid, Scarlett Johansson, and Blake Lively could offer to do you at once, and you'd refuse."

"Truth," he nodded. "But if you throw in Zendaya, I'd have to reconsider."

She mock-gasped. "You'd cheat? On me?" She slapped her arm against his chest, and he grabbed it. The warmth of his hand holding a part of her sent a sizzle across her skin. *Hello, hormones.* It didn't help his eyes relayed, "I want to devour you."

She pulled her arm free. She was driving, after all.

"You just can't stop touching me," he said.

His wicked grin did little to tamp down the frisson of heat between them.

She never felt like that—or talked like she did with him. Something about Theodore felt oddly safe and free at the same time. His teasing demeanor had her slip into sexy banter at the drop of a hat. It wasn't very professional, but it was fun.

Maybe she allowed the slip in decorum because his stay was temporary. Despite them saying they'd revisit their inconvenient chemistry *thing* on National BAE Day—whatever the hell that was—she knew the score. He was just a flirt.

Or maybe her willingness to cross boundaries was because she was still miffed as hell at her boss. She'd done everything he'd asked, and she'd gotten very little for it.

He leaned closer. "Listen, Roger's not going to say anything. His ego won't allow him to admit you weren't bowled over by him. Trust me. I'm a guy."

"I hadn't noticed."

"Let me take you to lunch. You can tell me all about what it's like at Edison Tech. Interview done, and *then* we return to the office."

Maybe she would let him interview her. She'd assure him her unwise out-of-the-office meetings with Roger were not romantic at all, despite the gossip. She'd lay out all the reasons she was an asset to Edison. Gathering some intel on Theodore herself wouldn't hurt, either.

She took him to Mrs. Meacham's Kitchen, a little cute bistro-set up in Georgetown. They parked in a nearby garage, and given it was 1:45, they easily found a table near the big window overlooking M Street. It was casual, and even better, no one from the office knew about the place—she hoped.

They ordered lunch. He chose a ham and cheese croissant sandwich and a glass of water, no ice. She went with her usual: an all-veggie salad and iced tea.

He tsked when the waitress put down her drink. "Again, the tea abomination continues."

She pushed the wrapper off the straw. "You don't have iced tea in England?"

"Wales. And yes. Sometimes. But no self-respecting place does. What did those tea leaves ever do to you to be treated so horribly?"

She snickered and dramatically dunked her straw into her iced tea and took a long draw. "Mmmm, *iced* cold tea."

"My taste buds are dying as I sit here." He lifted his water to his lips.

They sat in relative silence, sipping their drinks for a few minutes. His foot bumped hers, and a jolt of electricity went through her whole body. Time to shift to business talk —immediately.

Alice put her elbows on the table and her hands on her chin. "Okay, what do you want to know about my work?"

"Are you any good?"

She laughed. "Of course. But I'm sure all the girls tell you that."

"You wouldn't believe it."

The waitress arrived, put her salad in front of her and his sandwich before Theodore, then asked, "Get you folks anything else?" Her eyes remained glued to him.

"We're good, love. Thank you." He smiled up at her, and Gloria, as her nametag announced, paused. She gave him a wide smile and flushed.

Women regularly fell at his feet, didn't they? She wouldn't. Couldn't afford to.

She'd always been one to follow the rules, but he seemed to be a rule-breaker. That alone should have had her head for the hills.

She picked up her fork. "How did you get into this job anyway?"

Theodore dramatically snapped his napkin on his lap. "I got my MBA from University of Cambridge. Starting working for a manufacturing firm. Then, a tech firm. Turns out, in both places, I had a knack for ferreting out personnel problems. Discovering inefficiencies."

"So." She cleared her throat. "What do you do after you find these inefficiencies?"

"I report them to the higher-ups. They're the ones who make the decisions about who stays and who goes."

"And how does that make you feel?" God, she sounded like a psychologist.

He sighed, looking down at his hands. "Honestly? It's a mixed bag. On the one hand, I feel like I'm doing good work, making things better for everyone. But on the other hand, I know that some of the people I report on are going to lose their jobs. It's not easy."

She forked a piece of carrot. "Is this the part where I should feel sorry for you?"

"You think I like being the most hated person in a room? Making people cry?"

She gasped. "You make people cry?"

"Only sometimes." He waved his sandwich at her, then took a big bite.

"You could stop. Do something else."

"I like my work. I help companies. Basically, go in and show where things aren't working. The inefficiencies are—"

She held up her hand to stop him. "God, such corporate speak."

"Spoken by the accountant." He took another huge bite of his sandwich. The man really was hungry—and entirely wrong about her. The mere thought of using any of that jargon raised her internal temperature a few degrees.

She stabbed at her salad and stuffed lettuce in her mouth, not caring what she looked like. She was so sick of management types who didn't have to actually *do* the work, telling everyone how to do it better.

"Ya know," she said between chews. "It seems like the higher someone goes up the career ladder, their ability to see and know what's real lowers."

Like Roger. She remembered when he was a project manager. As soon as he was moved into the CEO position, his vague-speak went off the charts, and suddenly, he didn't know how to do anything. Tricia, too. She started out as a receptionist. Alice cheered when she was promoted but, still...

They all used the same words. Synergies. Inefficiencies. Redundancies. All words to make firing people more palpable. Roger, in particular, had been on a spree lately. And he thought Alice was getting ahead of her skis?

"Okay." Theodore brushed crumbs off his fingers. "Truth time. I ferret out the lazy people, the toxic ones, the people who make it harder on everyone around them. The people who are nice but don't really do anything. The people who are paid big money to basically show up to meetings and scroll through their phones while everyone else around them is making problems disappear. I make it possible for those lazy asses' salaries to be redistributed to those who are doing the work."

His vehement tone made her sit up. He clearly believed what he said.

"It never happens that way, though," she said.

"It should."

The man couldn't be that naïve. "But it doesn't."

"It at least has a chance," he sighed. "Even if it's hard trying to set things right."

Furrows formed between his eyes. Pain—that was what she saw in them. It must be hard to be the bearer of bad news. Perhaps that was why he always made jokes and was obsessed with throwing things off-kilter with National Iceberg Day or whatever.

It was impossible to not be a little charmed by the guy. There was something about a man with convictions and caring instincts that stirred warmth deep inside her.

The need to kiss him again arose—inexplicably. Her mouth watered as memories of the way he tasted crowded in on her, knowledge she shouldn't have. Snuggling up to a management consultant sent in to assess the staff—assess *her*? Yet she hadn't been able to push off him. In fact, her libido was still on fire around him. Even Roger's sudden appearance hadn't dampened a single, ignited, hormonal urge. Or her own conviction of getting that damned promotion if it were the last thing she did on earth.

The dichotomy in her mind and body was the oddest thing.

Get back to business, she reminded herself. "Roger and I had been talking about me being promoted to CFO, you know."

"I didn't know."

She slid her hands under her thighs and leaned forward. "Yep, but it hasn't materialized. Theodore, please tell me. How bad are things at Edison that the owners felt the need to bring you in? And is my job on the chopping block?" She might as well go there. Cutting personnel is the fastest way to curb expenses. Her lack of promotion also was making her suspicious. If she left Edison Tech, she wanted to leave on her own terms.

"Tell me why you want to keep it."

She straightened up, feeling a sudden surge of determination. "Because my work at Edison makes a difference. I've been working hard to improve the company's financial systems, and I think I've made a real impact." Even if Roger hadn't adopted most of her ideas, she knew things were better with her there.

He leaned back in his chair, studying her. "But that doesn't tell me why *you* want this job. What does it do for you?"

She hesitated, unsure how to answer. But his direct gaze, as if he was seriously interested, urged her to be truthful. "Making a difference is important to me, and I can at Edison. I have ideas for how we can improve our processes, if someone would listen."

"I'm listening." He picked up his sandwich and took another huge bite.

She started talking. If they made everyone submit their expense reports electronically with receipts attached, the new financial system she'd been eyeing would reconcile the two. Then, there was the matter of actually investing some of their cash flow instead of letting it sit in the corporate checking account. That last one was such a no-brainer, and she was shocked the company had never done it before. But Roger liked things to stay liquid.

The only thing she left out was how Roger also liked to spend—feasibility studies for new branding, new websites, all of which cost $25,000 a pop. Yet they never seemed to go anywhere. She'd questioned him about it, but he'd said it wasn't her department or concern.

Super prick.

Theodore listened intently to her ideas, his gaze only

breaking now and again to glance down at his rapidly disappearing lunch. He nodded and made little *hmm*ing noises as if he were actually taking in what she said. Her mind cleared even more, ideas popping in with gusto.

Like how buying the building that housed Edison Tech and leasing out unused parking spaces could raise money that could be reinvested into Research & Development and marketing.

She waved her fork. "R&D and marketing really needed a team building something-or-other because they're at each other's throats all the time."

"God, I hate those things." He chuckled. "Falling backward into people's arms. Rappelling down mountainsides on anchors and carabineers your colleagues put in. Though I suppose that's one way of getting rid of someone."

She nearly choked on her iced tea. "I would never let anyone at Edison be in charge of my anchors."

"Ah, and there's the truth." He pointed a finger at her. "The fact that you can't rely on them tells me everything. But I wouldn't let Roger near my rappelling gear, either, after this morning. I'd end up pancaked on the canyon floor."

"But he hired you." Roger had to think Theodore was the right man for the job.

"I was brought in by the owners. Roger had no choice. And that was before he heard me kissing you into oblivion. You, moaning out my name."

She flattened herself against her chair back. "I did not. I distinctly heard 'Alice ... Alice ... Oh, Alice.'" She fluttered her eyelashes.

"Can't blame a guy for that. Like I said, your kiss is ..." His gaze fell to her mouth.

She was far too interested in him finishing that sentence. My, how they reverted to flirting so quickly. And so often.

She threw down her napkin. "We need to get back to the office."

"You took the day off, remember?" His feet slid alongside one of hers, capturing it. She didn't pull back.

"I don't want to." Instead, she felt a burning need to accomplish something—something she could control. "I feel fine now, and I have a pile of work to do." She'd do it all from home.

"We have a lot in common, Alice."

"Oh?" She reached down to grab her purse and put it in her lap.

"We both work too much."

"Probably. Grab a cab or something so you go back to the office without me? So they won't think—"

"The office saw me carry you out."

Strong arms, his scent, all crashed back into her mind, and the heat between her thighs grew stronger. "Don't remind me. But I'm not going back to Edison. I'm going to work from my apartment. Someone said I should take the day off."

"Doesn't sound like you're doing that."

She shrugged. "Working from home feels like a vacation."

"Now, that's sad." He leaned forward a little, bringing his blue eyes closer to her. "When National BAE Day comes, I'm locking up your laptop and whisking you away."

She rolled her lips between her teeth, then let them out with a pop. "To where?"

"Where the office can't get to you."

They'd find her anyway. Most of the office had her cell phone on speed dial. "Is that what National BAE Day is about?"

"BAE stands for 'before anyone else'. It's an opportunity to show your lover they're truly number one in your life."

"Oh." Being number one to someone, and not just because

someone couldn't remember how to reboot the Wi-Fi, would be nice. "You celebrate every year?"

"Never have. Been wanting to, though."

Doesn't everyone want to find their one and only love? "It would be … nice."

Another one of his cocky smirks formed. "Nice? Oh, we'd be far better than that, Alice."

Shit, her panties were wet. "How do you know? What's happening here could be just pure chemistry. Nothing more."

"That's what we're going to disprove."

She swallowed. "By waiting until this made-up holiday."

"Not made up, but yeah," he said quietly.

They were going to have trouble delaying, weren't they? His foot still had hers captured. Her entire body was one giant vat of dancing hormones screaming at her. She *had* taken the day off. Would be a shame to waste it on something like laundry.

"Can I get you all anything else?" Gloria had magically appeared. She looked to Alice, then to Theodore, then back to Alice again. "Some pie, perhaps? It's National Pie Day somewhere today."

Alice drew in a long breath as her eyes locked on Theodore. He didn't take his gaze from her face, either. "No, thanks, Gloria. Just the check, please."

As soon as Gloria scooted away, Theodore leaned forward. "Alice, do you believe in signs?"

6

———————

Despite what he said at the restaurant, Theodore didn't believe in cosmic signs, fate, or soul mate rubbish. What he believed was that a certain part of his anatomy would explode before the end of the day if he didn't handle it. He'd prefer Alice did the handling, but he was beginning to see she was a woman of convictions.

He'd had his share of one-night stands, but they were all consensual, and that would never change. With Alice, however, they'd agreed to wait, so wait he would.

Then why were they standing outside her apartment door staring at one another, neither making the move to separate? He should go back to his rented apartment or Edison. She should get on with her weekend. But truth be told, neither of them felt like going back to work at 3:30 p.m. on a Friday.

Finally, she hitched a thumb toward her door. "This is me."

"I know."

"I don't believe in signs, by the way," she blurted, then captured her bottom lip between her teeth.

"Me, either." Though he'd given a little lecture on the car

trip over about how it was uncanny the waitress brought up Pie Day. She'd agreed. Then they'd been silent as if both internally wrestling with the idea of waiting. He knew he was. Five months without those lips again? His cock might actually fall off for the number of times it'd gotten semi-hard only to be deflated that day.

"You going back to work?" he asked.

She slowly shook her head. "No. In fact, maybe I should take off more weekends."

A smile raised his cheeks. It made him happy to know she was watching out for herself.

She got out her keys. "Have a great weekend."

She was dismissing him. "Maybe." A petulant childlike tone laced his voice. Bloody great. His cock must be speaking.

She tilted her head. "No plans? No interviews?"

"No."

"No, of course not. It's late on a Friday." Her bottom lip would be bruised to hell in minutes by the way her teeth kept grasping it. It made him want to reach out, cup her face, rescue it. Then devour her mouth with his own.

"Technically, I don't start until Monday."

Her chin jutted upward. "Oh? But our interview …"

"Was pure pleasure." He wasn't lying. He now had a good direction to go in for his employee interviews come Monday. She couldn't be the only one to see things were awry at Edison.

"So, you're not *really* starting until next week?" She leaned back against her front door, putting her hands behind her to cushion her back. It only made her breasts jut forward. If he didn't know better, he'd think she was trying to seduce him. Except she didn't need to try at all.

He scrubbed his hair as if that might bring blood back to his brain so he could think. It was hard to do around Alice, looking so delectable with glistening lips. "Didn't have any interviews set up for today. Except what we did at the restaurant, of course."

"We haven't had ours yet. Officially. It wasn't in the office." She rolled her lips between her teeth—again.

God, he needed to kiss her. "Okay, we'll have a do-over next week. When I'm officially—"

"Official?"

"Yes. Consider today an introduction day. The contract says I begin on Monday."

"Oh. That …"

"Changes things?" Even though getting romantically involved with another staff member was usually frowned upon by the owners of Edison, he couldn't help but yearn for a loophole in that unwritten company policy at that moment. Any thought about what he could lose—respect and maybe rank with his bosses—faded to black. Something about Alice had gripped him, and it wasn't letting go easily.

"It could. I mean …" She pushed off her sexy lean. "If we'd just met—"

"A boy and girl—"

"Running into one another by happenstance."

"In a snowstorm."

Her eyes warmed. "What would you have done if we had met that way?"

"I'd have asked you out. Maybe carried you if it snowed too much."

"You've already done that."

And God, he wanted to do it again. "Ah, but I didn't get to walk you to your door. Give you a proper, chaste kiss. Pray to the almighty you'd want to see me again."

She laughed a little at that.

He obliterated the last bit of space between them. "Would you have let me?"

"Kiss me? You've already done that, too."

"But not at the front door."

She threw her arms around him and mashed her body against him. Her lips sealed over his. *Ffyc*, she truly was spectacular at the kissing thing.

When she broke the lip lock, her lashes fluttered as if she'd surprised herself. "Was it any different?"

"Better." It was true. Every time she kissed him, it got better.

She tried to remove her arms, but he grabbed them and made her stay. "You don't believe in signs, but you believe in technicalities?"

She nodded. "Details matter. Especially around work, except we're not—"

"Working together yet. We're free to do what we want." Because really, hang what people thought. There was no legally binding or written policy they were breaking.

A slow smile crept across her face. He didn't know what else to do except bend his head to capture her lips again. His aching cock found the space between her legs where he would stay all weekend if she'd let him. His mind couldn't figure out how their fit happened, except Alice had semi-climbed up on him. Or maybe he'd lifted her up. His hands now clutched her bottom, holding her against him.

Who cared how they'd connected their bodies together like two interlocking puzzle pieces? His hands, his mouth, were full of her. And she clung to him with a physical desperation he'd never quite experienced. It egged him on.

"Keys," he growled into her mouth. They had to get inside, or nailing her against the wall in her apartment building's hallway was a genuine possibility. He'd never in his life needed to be inside a woman like her before.

Wrenching herself free, she twisted toward her door. His body stayed pressed against hers, his breath coming out in puffs against her hair as he nibbled on her neck. It made her keep missing the keyhole opening.

Finally, before he could take over, it slipped inside with a metallic rip. She got the door open, and he pushed her inside. She spun back into his arms, and he lifted her up so his cock could get back to its new favorite spot—right between her legs.

"We only do this during this weekend. That's it," she said into his mouth, killing his buzz immediately.

He put some distance between his face and her devil-blessed lips. "Oh? Using me for my body?"

"Mind?" She smiled up at him, and all thoughts of consequences cleared like smoke after a spring rain.

His hands were back on her, cupping her face. "Well, given this weekend has Make Your Dreams Come True Day …" he began.

A little giggle erupted from her throat. "What else does it have?"

"National Hot Pastrami Sandwich Day and Take a Missionary to Lunch Day."

"Missionary is my least favorite."

There was no mistaking her meaning. As for her declaration, they only had the weekend, and then it was back to business? He could do it. Their pull to one another was real —and if a technicality meant they could act on it and have her still feel good about it, who was he to disagree? The ball was in her court. She'd picked it up. He could play the game and see where it led. Risk be damned. "What's your favorite position?"

"All the others."

He ran a finger over his lips. "Could take all weekend."

"Well, I normally work on the weekends. But since I'm not CFO … *yet*." She took two steps backward and dropped her coat to the floor. "You have something better to do?"

"Better than making your dreams come true? I live for it."

"Or I make yours …"

The woman had confidence. It was an incredible turn-on.

He stalked forward, and she backed up the short hallway to her bedroom, where she kicked off her shoes and unbuttoned her shirt. "No work. No business talk this weekend."

"Agreed."

Alice was committed to her career, yes. But she also deserved to have a life. So far, from what he'd seen, she spent too much of it working. He traveled alone enough to realize connecting with people was far more important than a job—even if he sucked at the work-life balance himself.

He followed her lead, first draping his jacket across the back of an old wingback chair. Then, he yanked his tie free from his neck.

He, too, deserved something good when it was presented. He stalked forward.

~

The zing of Theodore's tie through his collar sent a cascade of sensation up Alice's legs, which had begun to quake.

Just inside her bedroom door, he stopped, leaving their faces mere inches apart.

His presence filled up the room, stealing all the oxygen. "You feel this, don't you?" His fingers circled her wrist, bringing her hand up to his chest, where he placed her palm against his heart. "What's between us?"

Alice nodded. Their chemistry was undeniable, and seeing if their pull to one another was real sooner than later was a good data point, right? Why wait months only to realize their attraction was an illusion? A big *can't-have thing* that grew and grew, only to disappoint once unleashed. Better to find out now.

And, a woman reserved the right to change her mind, right?

Plus, the only way she would fulfill her New Year's resolution was to do things differently than before. For once, she wouldn't spend the weekend staring at spreadsheets. And she was ready to take control—of one hot ginger.

Good self-pep talk, Alice.

Still, her logical side rose up. "Promise me this won't have anything to do with my job at Edison." She pulled her hand free and backed farther into her dark bedroom. The blinds were still pulled down, but it wouldn't have mattered. It may be only 4:30 p.m., but winter's early darkness was descending outside already.

He closed the distance between them again and cupped her face. "Your job evaluation will be based solely on your work performance. It will have nothing to do with what happens here." He brushed hair off her face, the tender move a dichotomy to the talk of work. Or maybe it was because his hands kept touching her, caressing her like stoking a low-burning fire.

He set his forehead against her. "Trust me."

"Everyone says that."

"But I mean it." His eyes blazed. "Did you know from the first time I saw you across that bar you got me hard?" His fingers played with the back of her neck.

Jesus. For a man who'd memorized made-up holidays like National Bobblehead Day and Museum Selfie Day, he knew how to turn the goofball off—and turn on the seduction.

She snuck a peek down at his crotch. Theodore Gaston the Fourth would be … What in bed? She really wanted to know. So far, he had the touching thing down pat.

"I like your hands," she said.

"They like you." It didn't take long for him to have her

backed up against her bed, where the sheets were still in a tangled mess from the night before.

His gaze dropped to her breasts, now free of the blouse. Thank God, she'd worn one of her laciest bras. That morning, hungover and in a hurry to get to work, she'd grabbed one from the back of the drawer because all her everyday ones were in the laundry.

"Now"—his hands drifted down her arms and to her back. He released her bra, which slipped down between them —"let me appreciate your assets."

His hands moved to her breasts. Keeping his gaze on her face, he cupped them, thumbing her nipples. She sucked in a breath. One little move had her entire body ready, willing, and able to have him do whatever he wanted.

She reached for his belt buckle, earning a half smile from him. After shedding the rest of their clothes, he pressed himself against her, his lips dusting across hers. She fell back on the bed, and he immediately covered her. His mouth fell to her breast, and he tenderly sucked on one nipple, then moved to the next. "Mmm, assets, indeed."

While he feasted on her, she ran her fingers through his red-gold hair, soft and silky. He had good hair. Patty would be proud; though no way would she let her friend near his head. My, how easily she'd begun to feel possessive of him.

His gaze flicked up for one second. "January 2. National Breast Appreciation Day. As if I'd wait for that day to come around again after tasting"—his gaze again dropped—"these."

She giggled.

He moved up her clavicle, nibbling his way up to her ear. "Alice. Touch me." He leaned on one elbow, grabbed her hand, and brought it down to his ... *Sweet Jesus on high.* Her fingers curled around him. She was about to have the greatest sex of her life, wasn't she?

He let out a long hiss as her fingers moved. "So, all the positions?"

She nodded, speech abandoning her.

"Then hang on." He circled his arm around her back, rolled, and pulled her on top of him. His cock was now trapped between her belly and him. "I rather love this one. Gives me access to your"—his hands cupped her breasts again—"spectacular assets."

Rising, she straddled him. "No more talking."

He arched an eyebrow. "Bossy."

"Needy."

His eyes darkened, his jaw tensing. "Even better."

He rolled over, reached for his trousers, and found a condom. He had it on in a second, which was good because her mind might have spun in all directions that he was so prepared.

When he turned back to her, the quip on her tongue about what a good boy scout he must've been, died. The blue in his eyes burned with desire.

She kicked off her panties and scrambled back onto him, earning herself a low rumble from his chest.

He grasped her hips and positioned her, and she sunk down on him. All the air in her lungs escaped, and a satisfying moan came from his throat.

"Ffyc, you're so hot and tight."

He was big, and she could feel him fill every inch inside her body. She pitched her hips forward, seeking the best spot. His torso contracted, and he grunted. She did it again. And again. And every time, his nostrils flared; his lids dropped.

He grasped her rib cage, pulled her down toward him so their faces were inches apart. "I need your mouth when you ride me."

So, she obliged. Kissed him hard and deep as her hips

circled and pitched into him until they panted like animals in heat. His tongue kept sliding into her mouth just at the right time, and she sucked on it. Needing more. Always more.

She usually wasn't a rough and tumble girl, but with Theodore, she wanted to devour him—and have him do the same to her. Any thought of what they were doing, what they *should* do or not do was as distant as China.

The slap of flesh and moans filled the room, and she was sure her bed was moving so much she was destroying the wall behind it. As if that would make her stop.

He moved from kissing her mouth to her breasts and back to her mouth again so many times; her entire body was on fire—a bonfire.

"Alice," he hissed. "Clench hard around my cock. That's right, baby. So damned good." So much for the cliched British uptight mannerisms.

But she did it. Again and again, she gripped him with her insides. Each time, he responded. She could grow addicted to that—the power that came from making a man come undone.

Just the thought of it created new sensations, and she was suddenly coming—hard. As she was touching down, she felt him twitch inside her, his own release on its heels.

She fell to his chest, lying there as his rib cage expanded with each lungful of air, making her rise and fall on him.

After his breath steadied, his arms wrapped around her. He murmured into her hair, "You're an animal in bed, Alice Crawford."

A burst of giggles … She didn't know why she found that funny. Her laughter couldn't be stopped, however. Her? An animal?

She lifted her head to stare at him. "Oh, yeah, I'm an insatiable sex pot."

"Lucky me." He put one of his arms behind his head. His

hair was a tousled mess and adorable. His hand reached out, and he ran his fingers across her chin. "You got some 'stache rash from my beard."

She ran her palm over his significant five o'clock shadow. It looked good on him. Like a rugged highlander. *Like a Jamie Fraser.* "Worth it."

"Wait till it's all over your thighs. Then it'll be worth it." He rolled her off him, settled onto his side. "How much time do you need?"

She blinked. "Time?"

His fingers drifted down her bare hip, dipped in between her legs. "Just getting started, love."

Theodore Gaston the Fourth was a god.

7

———————

Theodore's eyes snapped open. For one long minute, he couldn't recall where he was. Not unusual for him, given he woke up in a different hotel room or rental nearly every week.

A very soft, female body was snuggled up against his back, and a wash of warmth ran over his skin. A soft murmur followed.

Alice.

He'd been balls deep inside her half the night. The mere memory got him hardening. He twisted to face her. "Hey there. Dream of me?"

Her eyes grew wide, and she gasped. She scrambled to sit up, knocking into him, and cold air hit him as he slipped from under the sheet. Arms whirling, he fell backward to the roughest carpet his skin had ever had the displeasure of connecting with. "Ffyc me."

Alice rubbed at her eyes. "Oh, sorry."

He coughed a little, jumping up. "Good God, that's a first."

"You're naked." Clutching the sheet to her breasts, her

eyes glanced down at his morning half-mast. "And truly a redhead."

"Truly. What's this carpet made of? Gravel?"

"Again, sorry, you surprised me. I … forgot it was you. I often wake up not knowing where I am. Even at home. And usually alone, and …"

Ah, so they had that in common, as well. But forget he was there? "Wound my ego, will ya?" He grinned. "Got to say, that's the first time a woman's kicked me out of bed. Especially after I made her eyes roll back into her head. More than once."

She scoffed at him. "What time is it?" Her hands slapped around as if searching for something. "Where's my phone?"

Hell if he knew where his own mobile was, let alone hers. He stretched his neck. "Probably with your clothes. Abandoned in the living room. Ripped from your body like a wild animal."

She smirked. "Are you trying to make me feel slutty?"

"Are you into that?" He scooted back on the bed. "Because if you are, I can—"

She rose to her knees, clutching the sheet, and slapped his bicep, rather hard.

He rubbed his arm. "Ow. Please tell me you aren't a sadist."

She inched her way to the other side of the bed, yanking the sheet around her and then stood. "No, I must be a masochist because we"—she waggled her finger between them—"had a deal. Broke it. Then made a new deal because I was mad at my boss, wanted—"

"A good shag?"

"More of a life. Shit, I didn't go back to the office. And you didn't go back. And *we didn't establish the counter story …*" She clung to the sheet and stared up at him, slack-jawed.

The woman was truly horrified and, quite frankly, giving him whiplash. One minute, she was a seductress, and the next, she was one step away from joining a convent.

"They'll think what they think." He knew enough about office politics and gossip. Neither could be contained. "Besides, it's a little late for us to be overanalyzing things. Although, what I'm thinking right now …" Her taste still sat on his tongue.

"*Theodore.*" She dropped her face in her hands. "What was I thinking?"

"Alice." He held out a hand, palm up. "We didn't do anything wrong."

"I know," she bit out. "But what do we know about each other really? Like, who are you?"

"Theodore Gaston the Fourth."

She threw a pillow at him, which at least didn't give him rug burns like the ones he sported on his ass.

He chuckled, sat back down on the bed, stuffed the thing behind his head, and leaned back against the headboard. "I'm thirty-five, have one brother, wanted to be a professional footballer when I grew up, and believe Hermione should have ended up with Harry."

She gasped. "But Ron is a ginger."

"We don't run in packs, you know. It's also important to know I believe Britney Spears was done dirty by her family." He snapped his fingers. "Also, I'm also partial to smart women who really should have any job they want in life, especially if they're clearly qualified for it."

His words earned a small smile from her.

"Now, get your spectacular breasts back into this bed. I have more adoring to do."

She lifted her chin. "Spectacular, huh?"

"Yes. You think they're all worshipped out?" He put his

hands behind his head. "Unless last night was a dream, and I was merely hallucinating …"

She dropped the sheet and stood there, nude, in glorious defiance.

"Remind you of anything?" She grinned widely.

The woman was something. Uptight and far too worried what other people thought, but she had gumption. "Many things, actually."

"I don't usually do this." She placed her hands on her hips. "But you're on team Britney, so …"

"So?"

"So, so much for staying *north of your privates*, as you said." She waved her hands toward his crotch.

"We couldn't help ourselves. You're too hot, and I'm too adorable."

She snorted, then slapped her hands across her mouth.

"You're right. Adorable is too soft—" he pitched his torso and let his growing erection bob in her direction—"of a word for me and my state."

"But on Monday, we go back to work and our original plan. And you'll think no less of me. And I won't out you, either."

"As we decided. No time for second thoughts now." He patted the bed next to him. "Besides, I wouldn't want to be treated to your vengeful side, though, feel free to use me as a big eff-you to the corporate life that expects you to have no life outside of it."

"You're my knight in shining armor." She batted her eyelashes.

He tapped the place next to him. "Time's a wasting. I only have thirty-six hours left to introduce you to *my* favorite position."

She finally sat back down on the bed. "What's that?"

"I'll tell you when we're in it."

He leaned forward to kiss her, and she climbed on top of him. It took them another hour to even consider leaving her bed before finally landing in the shower. He'd also never taken one so long before—until they were both pruny and spent. He only hoped the neighbors weren't too upset by the noise—mostly from Alice. Tile was a natural megaphone.

8

———————

Hand in hand, they slowly strolled around the Jefferson Memorial. They'd stopped at his rented condominium so he could get clean clothes. It was a battle to not fall back into his bed, but Alice was proud of her resolve. He didn't push the issue, either. Rather, he suggested a walk and a little sight-seeing—preferably where they wouldn't run into anyone they knew, he'd offered. She appreciated his discretion and the time to move her sore limbs. Their night had been acrobatic.

"I can't believe you haven't been here," Alice said as they made their way along the edge of the tidal basin. The Jefferson Memorial Park was almost empty. Then again, in January, it wasn't exactly a hot spot for most people. "How many times have you been to DC again?"

"Four. Never got farther than a block from any of the hotels."

"That's some dedication to work."

She liked that about him. She was beginning to like a lot of things about him. Like how he walked on the outside, closest to the road, but then switched his position when they got close to the water as if to shield her from falling in. Maybe being with him like that wasn't a bad idea.

For one, his skills in the bedroom were off the charts. Looking at him, she would have thought he'd be wound as tight as Big Ben's winding mechanism. Rather, he was the opposite. Free and open. Ravenous in his sexual appetite.

He lifted his face up to the sun. "Nice day. Almost like spring."

She laughed. "It's forty degrees." Thank God the warmth from his hand was keeping her digits from falling off. At least the snow had melted. Nothing but a few piles of sooty slush was left here and there.

"Where I come from, this is like spring."

She'd die. "You really have to visit when the cherry blossoms are in full bloom. It's like snow falling all around you." She'd only made it down to the tidal basin during blooming season one time a few years ago, but it was one of her most favorite things she'd done since moving to DC five years ago.

"I'll put that on the list. For April 18. It's International Day for Monuments and Sites."

She slowly shook her head. "How do you remember all those?"

He tapped his forehead. "Photographic memory."

She stopped short, her hand slipping from his. "Seriously?"

"Truly." He grasped her hand again, which was good because, unlike her companion with his thick British skin, she immediately began to shudder.

He must have felt it because he lifted her hand to his mouth and huffed hot air over her skin. To think she thought the man was as strange as one got a few days ago. Now, her panties couldn't stay dry around him.

"You're a surprise, Theodore."

He winked at her. "You, too, Alice. Let's learn more surprising things about one another."

He drew her to a bench, swiped his hand over it, then gestured for her to sit with him.

They stared silently for a few minutes over the dirty basin water and the ducks gliding along the edge. She wanted to ask him questions but didn't know where to start. The cold air did little to wake up her brain—except for one thing. Theodore had said his ex-girlfriend married his ex-best friend. That had to have been tough.

She curled her fingers around his hand. "I do have one question for you."

"Fire away."

"What happened between you and your ex-girlfriend?" She watched his face closely to see if she'd crossed a line.

His jaw tensed a little. "Hmm. Hard story."

She pulled her hand free, then clutched them in her lap. "I shouldn't have asked."

He shrugged. "It's okay. Just no easy answer there. I traveled a lot. She got lonely. My best mate was there."

There was more to this story, wasn't there? "But your friend…"

She shouldn't be pushing it, but you could tell a lot about a guy based on their past romantic relationships. She had questions. Like, how long were they together? Did he love her? Did she cheat? Or did they break up, and then she went off with this "ex-best mate"?

None of it was her business, considering they'd known each other for mere days. But her curiosity was growing about him, and they *had* seen every inch of each other naked. That had to qualify for some level of life intimacy, right?

When Theodore didn't answer, she studied his face and decided to drop it. Except he then answered her anyway. "He cared for her more than for me. But I wasn't a saint, either. I didn't alleviate her fears about my travels; though she had nothing to worry about. Got sick of her questioning me all the time. Got tired of hearing I loved the airport more than her." He angled his body to face her. "What about you?"

"What about me? I don't date that much."

The whole office at Edison Tech saw her more than anyone else. Her career had always been the most important thing to her—at least until that weekend.

"Surprising."

"You really haven't been out and about in DC much. It's not exactly the land of romance." Rather, a perfect place to put your job center stage. It was why she'd moved there, away from her little hometown of Junction Pine, where no one ever lived farther than ten miles from their families or sometimes never even got past tenth grade in their schooling. She knew by the time she was seven years old that wouldn't be her life.

"Then how did you get so good at kissing?"

A sliver of pride ran through her. But he'd been honest with her; she'd be honest back. "Meredith Lane. My best friend in seventh grade."

His head fell back. "Jesus, you're getting me hard again."

"No, no. She taught me how to practice on a peach. She said all the boys were trying to grow those little soft mustaches"—she waved over her lip—"and it would help neutralize the tickling if we got used to it. I must have gone through a bushel of them that summer."

"August 27. National Peach Day. I will never think about it the same way again."

"What about you? How'd you get so good at ..." Her thighs were a little raw from his beard.

"Worshipping? I never kiss and tell." He lifted her hand to his lips.

"That's good because we're not telling anyone anything."

She may be okay with how the weekend had unfolded, but that didn't mean she'd ever be comfortable with the whole world knowing her business.

"What could I say anyway? That you've made me rethink not only National Peach Day but how, this year, I *really* want to celebrate National Work Naked Day—"

"You made that one up." She pulled her hand free, but he grasped it again. They then started a little hand tug-of-war like little kids.

"February 7," he said. "And I still say we call in sick on Monday and work from home and—"

"Get nothing done?" Her hand landed on his chest, and he held it there.

"We'd get a lot done, my little freak in the spreadsheets." He began to push her hand lower down his torso.

"I am committed to always doing a good job, no matter what that entails." Her fingers connected with his belt buckle, and there went another pair of panties. At that point, she'd have to do laundry every day to keep up with how many she'd cycle through in twenty-four hours.

"Oh, I see that. In fact, I say we go get some peaches, and you show me exactly what I've been missing in the food porn area."

Her laughter was interrupted by someone calling her name. A woman in a bright red coat was making her way to them. Oh, shit. It was Patty.

Alice swung her gaze to Theodore. "Remember. Nothing happened."

"Alice!" Patty closed the distance and slapped her hands on the back of the bench, a little out of breath. "I thought that was you."

Patty smiled at Alice, glanced at Theodore, then back at her. Her eyes narrowed. "What nothing happened?"

So much for the Tidal Basin in January being a good idea.

9

———————

"Patty?" Alice blinked at her friend as if she were a figment of her imagination. Hard to do, given her crimson-colored coat stood out like a cardinal against the last bits of snow and brown trees behind her. Running into someone you knew, let alone a friend from work, was almost unheard of in the city.

"Alice," Patty blinked, her tone cautious. Probably because she stood frozen like a scared rabbit. She didn't count on meeting anyone she knew with Theodore in tow.

"What are you doing here?" Instant regret filled her for sounding so accusatory. It wasn't Patty's fault Alice was out with their company's new management consultant.

"Meeting Steph. She's never seen the Jefferson before. Can you believe it?" Patty moved forward. "Then we're going to the Mall to throw snowballs at hot men. It's the new flirting. So, taking a little romantic stroll around the monuments?" She eyed Theodore up and down, who had stood up when Patty got near.

Theodore grinned back at her. "Yes, Alice thought I should see—"

"Oh, no. Just taking a walk, and we ran into each other—"

Her and Theodore's words ran over each other in a mad gush.

Shit, shit, shit. Patty was no fool. She had a radar for two things: lies and sex. Her face practically reflected all the things Alice and Theodore had done the last two days. Things she wanted to keep to herself.

Alice cleared her throat and rose. "I mean—"

"We talked about—" Theodore started.

"At the *office*—"

"My ex-girlfriend and—"

"How DC—" Would the man shut up already?

"Has so many monuments—"

Jesus, Theodore. "That he'd never—"

"And then peaches came up—"

"Stop, stop." Patty held up her hand, then twirled her finger in the air. "First, these are cherry trees, not peach trees. What's really going on?"

Theodore's smile grew even wider. "Damn. Caught." He was having fun with it. Didn't he get it? Patty worked at Edison Tech. She knew everyone and everything, and even though she was Alice's friend, them being out together on a Sunday did not look good. Not at all.

"You can stop trying to make something up." Patty drew closer. "Now, quick. Before Steph gets here. One, is this real love or a fling? And two, what counter-story do you want me to plant?"

Oh, thank God. Alice smacked Theodore in the chest with the back of her hands. "I knew it. Patty's got our back."

Theodore grabbed her arm and held it. "We don't know yet."

Patty crossed her arms. "Know? We need to come up with something. Fast."

Theodore continued to hold Alice's arm. His touch was not helping the situation.

"No, I'm answering your question," he said. "Real love or a fling. We don't know yet."

Alice withdrew from his hold and slowly swung her head his way. "It's a little early—"

"To call it? Yes, I agree. We'll have to see on National BAE Day."

Patty raised her eyebrows. "What?"

Alice waved her hand. "It's a day where lovers celebrate their one and only. Like 'before anyone else'?"

Patty's eyebrows nearly touched the clouds. "Are you serious? Here? The land of men married to their cell phones and laptops?" She scoffed, her breath a silver cloud hanging in the air.

"And here I thought you were the cynical one," Theodore muttered to Alice.

The man was so naïve. Alice turned her attention back to Patty. "The truth is, we have a … chemistry thing here. And we needed to assess it, ya know, and talk about it. Sort it out."

Patty half smiled and nodded slowly. "Jamie Frasier did it again. Completely smothered any sense out of a woman."

She had that one right. Then again, she was allowed to have a life, right? Look what focusing solely on work had gotten her. A stuck career. No radar for who was flirting and who wasn't. Hello, Roger. At least Theodore was up front about his intentions.

"Well, we have to come up with something pronto," Patty said. "After you left? There was *talk*. And Roger was being … himself." She rolled her eyes.

Great. The rumor mill had already started about them. Why did she have to faint? And why did Theodore catch her? In front of everyone, to boot.

Alice swallowed. "Talk? Like what?"

"Tricia and Steph think you have a crush on Theodore." As if on cue, a dog barked in the background.

Alarm bells went off inside her. Having a life outside of work didn't mean everyone got to have a say in it. "I *do not*. Sorry, Theodore," she added quickly.

An annoying twinkle formed in his eyes. "I wouldn't call it a crush. More like …"

Before he could say anything else, because clearly the man had no sense of self-preservation, she held up both hands. "We need your help, Patty. To avoid suspicion. But first, is something going on?"

"Something set off Roger."

Double shit. The last thing she needed was for Roger to be upset, especially after too many people watched Theodore carry her out of the lobby, and Roger found them together at her apartment.

Patty straightened her glasses, and cleared her throat. "Okay, before we create this false story—and I know it's false so don't argue with me about it"—she pointed at Alice— "here's the current situation at work, the environment in which this counter-story will be spread. The office was a total mess when you two didn't come back. Technically, when *Alice* didn't come back."

"What happened?"

"Harrison's car wouldn't start again," Patty continued. "So, thank God you left the jumper cables, but no one seemed to know how to work them, and then when we got back in, Roger was muttering and kicking things—"

Theodore's twinkling ended. "Kicking?"

"A big shipment of paper came in, and the storeroom's full, and no one knew where to put it, so it's in the hall-way, which is what got Roger bumping into things. He literally kicked a box until it split open. He was muttering something about The Twins coming down next week and not knowing what people are really like and—"

Alice gasped. "The Twins? Come down? You mean"—she pointed her finger up and then down—"they're leaving their penthouse view in New York to visit us?"

Suzy and Samuel O'Flannery weren't technically twins. Rather, they were a brother and sister team that hit it big in the heyday of the internet bubble in the early 2000s as prodigal teenagers. In fact, they made so much money on their first venture that they could separately fund several new companies. It became a game for them, trying to one-up each other until they called a truce and formed Edison Tech and several other companies around the world together.

The staff saw them exactly once a year—the annual St. Patrick's Day party. They stayed for thirty minutes and drank one green drink developed for the event. Last year, it was a horrid Girl Scout cookie concoction with real crumbled-up Thin Mints over whipped cream drizzled with crème de menthe. Alice's stomach clenched as she remembered it.

Theodore rocked back on his heels. "It was bound to happen. They own the company."

Of course, Theodore would know that. In fact, he'd probably met them already. But they really needed to focus on the issue at hand because Patty had more to say.

"Then, the copier"—Patty dropped her voice a whisper—"the Big Whale? Wouldn't work." She lifted her gaze to Theodore. "The copier is in love with Alice and only works when she's in the building. That really put Roger in a tizzy."

Theodore pursed his lips. "A copier? People still need those?"

"We do, and it needs Alice."

"She does have a special touch." He grinned down at her.

Patty's eyes softened. "Aww, that's sweet."

"Patty." Alice snapped her fingers in front of her friend's doe-eyes. "I can deal with all that later." She took in a large breath and blew it out, praying to God what she was about to tell Patty didn't backfire on her. "What you don't know is Roger showed up at my place on Friday afternoon after Theodore drove me home. He assumed certain things."

Patty's mouth dropped to an O, and then she stared up at Theodore. "You really are a Jamie." She practically sighed the words at him. But then she raised her chin. "Okay. Spill it. What's going on with you two? Start with after the big fainting episode. Yes, I heard about it."

Everyone likely had. Theodore glanced Alice's way but wisely didn't address her humiliating moment in the lobby.

Alice clasped her hands together. "Theodore drove me home. We were talking at my apartment when Roger showed up," Alice filled in. "Theodore made me … tea."

"I did *not*." He scowled. "There was nothing that resembled *tea* in that apartment." He turned to Patty. "Then after retrieving her car from the impound lot—"

"Impound?"

"It was still stuck from Thursday night's snowstorm. It'd been towed, and thanks to this country's adherence to the capitalist regime, we were able to liberate it for the bargain price of seven hundred dollars."

Patty's eyebrows were in the clouds now. "You went with her?"

"Of course. Have you ever been to that section of town? One would need nunchucks and a German Shepherd to get out alive. Then I took her to lunch, which, again, had no proper tea, I might add." It appeared Patty wasn't the only drama queen.

Patty leaned toward him. "You got a brother, Theodore?" If Alice didn't know better, little invisible hearts were floating out of Patty's chest.

"He's married."

"How about an uncle? Aging father who looks like you?"

"Patty!" Alice couldn't watch the back and forth with the two of them anymore. The clock was ticking.

"Right. My entire future, including the children I'm going to have with someone from his chivalrous bloodline, can wait. We need to decide how to handle this. If Roger found you at home with Theodore … *man*." She glanced at Theodore. "He's a bit paranoid, you see. Always thinking someone is talking about him behind his back, which is ironic as hell, given what he does."

Theodore inched closer to her. "What do you mean?"

Okay, regaining control of the situation just turned critical. She grasped her friend's elbow and moved her to the bench. "We're sitting. In case Steph walks up, it's just you and me. We ran into each other. And Theodore … go…" she waved her hand. "… over there."

"No," Patty whined. "He needs to know the story, too."

"He knows it already. As he said, on Friday, we got my car and then went to lunch and began our interview." No need to talk about the ensuing thirty-six hours.

"And after?" She winked. "The interview continued? Inventoried all your, um, skills?" she whispered.

"Patty!" She was getting tired of screaming the woman's name.

"Okay, okay." Patty shook her head as if clearing her mind. "You can fill me in on the salacious details later."

Absolutely not. "Nothing to tell."

"Uh, huh. Sure, there isn't. And what about Roger? What happened when he showed up?" Her eyes grew wide and her spine straightened as her hands clutched in two fists at her chest. "He was boss interruptus? Was there a duel? A fight for your honor? Dammit, and I missed it." She stomped her foot.

Patty's theatrics were at an all-time high. "Nothing like that. He was just checking on me."

"His ego demanded to check in on her," Theodore said, still not walking away.

"He does have a big one, and yes, I know all about you being Miss December, Alice, even if you didn't let me in on it. I forgive you, by the way." Patty raised one eyebrow.

Theodore's brows furrowed. Great, she had to bring that up. Alice sighed. She didn't want to revisit her unwise decision to have dinners with Roger, even if under the guise of work.

"Can you tell people tomorrow morning that you talked to me and I'm fine now? After Theodore and I had an interview lunch, he brought me back to my apartment." Technically true. He just stayed. "You can say I spent the weekend in bed." Also true, just with Theodore.

Patty's smile returned in full force, and she nodded knowingly. "Because you weren't feeling well?"

"You can say that." A tiny lie. It wasn't her fault National Pie Day was mentioned by the waitress and sent them into thinking it was kismet or something. It *was* her fault, however, for getting them to try out all the sexual positions she could think of for the ensuing thirty-six hours.

Guilt and a zing of satisfaction warred inside her. She wasn't sorry about finally having some fun. Not even now after defying all statistical probability by immediately running into a coworker friend out of 5,490,000 people in the greater Washington, DC, area. Getting caught wasn't something she'd ever believed could happen. So much for being in control.

She took her friend's hand. "You didn't see me or hear from me until right here, where I sat with you. Only you." Also factual. Theodore remained standing.

"True. We *sat* together. Theodore is not on the bench."

Alice always knew people underestimated Patty's cleverness. "And on Monday, Theodore is launching into his set of interviews, which you are very much looking forward to, right?"

She nodded vigorously. "Oh, yes. Very much. Bring a family tree of all the single men in your family, Theodore. So." She slapped her lap. "I see Steph over there, so run away, you two. I got the story." She rose and held out her hand, which Alice took. "Good and done."

"Good and done," Alice repeated and began to push Theodore away. "Let's go, let's go, let's go."

Theodore shook his head. "You two scare me."

Alice grabbed his arm and pulled him away. Right then, she realized the whole story they concocted could have been done over the phone. They could have made a clean getaway before Steph even showed. Something about Theodore made her lose all sense, which was not her usual state.

When they were a safe distance away, meaning Patty and Steph were nowhere to be seen, she stopped short. "I want you to know I don't fabricate stories like that. But this is a unique circumstance." Her breath came out in puffs. The temperature had to have dropped another ten degrees since they'd been outside.

"I get it. But why do you do all those things?" His too-blue eyes bore into her.

A breeze blew hair in her face, which she angrily swiped away. "Do what?"

"Jumper cables, storeroom inventory, copier maintenance."

She rubbed her hands together. "That's all you're worried about? We almost got *caught*, Theodore." How could he not see the danger ahead? A small throb began behind her left eye.

"And what's this about Miss December?"

Her belly twisted. "It's nothing." *Please don't ask me about that*, she silently begged. It was humiliating enough she'd been so blind to Roger's ways, bouncing from one woman to another. It was a whole other mortifying scenario that people thought she was one of them.

Then again, he'd linger at her office door when she worked late and brought her doughnuts in the morning. How could she have not seen his motives? He *was* flirting all that time.

She'd picked the right New Year's resolution, and she was exercising it right now.

"We can't do this." She swished a finger between them. "Ever again. It's too dangerous."

"Oh?" His lips thinned, his features stilling.

"This … was a mistake. Huge, actually."

"I see." His mouth set in a hard line, his tone sharp as a stiletto. "And to think I've been accused of putting work over everything else."

Oh. Maybe she'd hurt him. What man didn't want his conquests to be fawned over, especially by the woman involved? But Theodore didn't seem the type to need his ego stroked *that* much. And he'd started it all. Sort of.

She reached for his arm, but he pulled it away. "I meant—"

"I know what you meant, Alice. And you're right. I should prepare for tomorrow. See you around." He spun away.

She stared at his back, and her heart split in two. One half jumped for joy that they were going to go back to their original plan: Be all business until June 10 when it was National BAE Day. She understood a plan. The other half, however? Crumbled to dust by his cold turn.

She sucked in a long cold breath that nearly froze her lungs. The whole scene was absurd. She'd known the man for mere days. Granted, they'd done things she'd never done with anyone, but still … They'd *done things*.

Maybe they just fizzled out?

She shook her head a little as if that would make her brain gain some sense. "I should probably go to Edison, too," she called after him. If that was how he wanted to play it, she wouldn't stop him.

He turned in profile. "No, you should go home. I'll take the office."

Oh, he was delineating territory already, was he? Before she could argue, he marched away. With every step, the side of her heart that was Team Theodore beat louder and louder. But she held her ground, watching his broad back, his long strides taking him away from her. Her pride demanded she not run after him. Instead, she stood there, stupidly pining for … what?

Alice's romantic experience was pretty minimal. A high school boyfriend she gave her virginity to. A college boyfriend who studied chemistry and was far too into edibles to make bedtime antics wild. A few dates here and there after school and fumbling a few times in one or two of their beds in their cramped suburban apartments after a wine festival in Southern Maryland or a day of bar hopping in Georgetown. How boring it all seemed now that she'd spent time with Theodore.

But she was a big girl, and, actually, running into Patty could've been a gift. Fun times were over. She had a promotion to secure.

10

———

Roger's aftershave entered her office before he did. He leaned against her doorframe, picking lint off his jacket. It looked new. He always was a clothes horse.

"Something I can do for you?" She set her bag down and shrugged off her coat.

"Only getting in now?" He glanced at his watch. "I trust you rested up over the weekend."

Jesus, it was only 9:10 a.m. "I picked up Patty. Her car wouldn't start. And I'm fine. Everything's fine." *Not.* "I spent the weekend in bed." Dammit, she flushed from head to toe. Probably because she'd spent most of the weekend between the sheets and not getting much rest.

One of his eyebrows lifted. "Good. Listen, I was thinking about our last conversation."

Damn. She really hoped he'd forget all about showing up at her apartment Friday and finding Theodore. She was trying hard to.

He closed the door behind him, and great, he—and his cologne—stepped in closer to her. She'd have to breathe through her mouth or risk a huge sneezing attack.

"I have a project for you. A test run, so to speak," he said.

Her heart skipped a beat. "A test?"

He plunked himself down in the chair next to her desk. She really might suffocate. "You want to be CFO, well, then I'd like an asset management plan."

Oh. That was something she'd wanted to do for some time. "I'd love to." Maybe Roger hadn't completely ruled her out as a potential CFO. "It will take some time."

He waved his hand. "Take all the time you need. But first," —he leaned down, placed his elbows on his knees, stared up at her—"the O'Flannerys are dropping in this afternoon."

"I heard." She leaned back in her chair as if that might put some distance between her nose and his cloud of scent.

He straightened. "You did? Where?"

"Oh. I can't remember. Probably overheard it in the kitchen?" She would not out Patty because, while Roger enjoyed gossip, he didn't like anyone else who did. Which was so ironic if she thought about it.

"It's terrible timing," Roger continued. "And with you being out this weekend, we didn't get to prepare for today. I trust you have those reports for me."

She swallowed a second "sorry," though guilt crept up on her. It made her a little angry she was even feeling guilty. He was the man who thought she moved too fast—on skis. "Uh, in a few minutes. What do the O'Flannerys want to see?"

"Not sure. They called it a drive-by." Roger fidgeted, kept clearing his throat. "But I suppose you should prepare the usual financial reports, the P&L, etc."

"Of course. Any thoughts on the discrepancies I found? Did you see what I flagged last week?" Things weren't adding up in marketing expenditures. A few expenses were connected to vendors she'd never heard of before. It wasn't the first time—seeing inconsistencies and bringing them up to Roger. He always told her he had it handled.

And unless she brought a sleeping bag into the office, she didn't have time to do a deep dive on her own. The books eventually went into the black again; though their profits were marginal at best.

Maybe that was why the O'Flannerys were stopping by? The Twins were legendary for having a golden touch when it came to making money.

He raised an eyebrow. "As I told you, things are always up and down in business. But"—he leaned closer—"I don't need to tell you that discretion about financial matters is key."

"Of course." What was he getting at?

He stood up and slapped her desk once. "I have more projects for you, too. Ideas to implement. Even some of yours."

There was an insult in there somewhere, but she batted it away in her mind. A sliver of hope rose instead. "Does this mean I'm still in the running for CFO?" She'd keep asking until he told her no.

He blew out a breath through his nose. "Ambitious as ever, I see."

"My career is important to me. Edison is important," she added quickly.

"Yes, yes, of course. In due time. If things go well."

Her heart did a little happy dance. Oh, they would go well if she had anything to do with it. "Those reports won't take me long. I'll bring them to you."

He left, leaving her door open (thank God). She blinked, her head swimming a little from the cloud of aftershave over her entire office.

She turned to her laptop, but Theodore's laughter from somewhere in the office reached her ears. Probably charming the panties off yet another unsuspecting female as he had hers.

Had she always been that easy when it came to men? No, she had not.

Was she sorry she had a great weekend full of multiple orgasms? No, she was not.

Then why did a dark cloud settle in her chest? She was the one who'd put distance between them. Things had worked out the way she'd wanted, right?

And, honestly, she'd just heard she was in the running for her *dream job*. People did crazy things to try to work for an O'Flannery company, according to *Executive Suite* magazine, which did a huge piece on them and their successes last year.

Like the guy who reportedly sent different kinds of gourmet coffee from around the world to java addict Samuel O'Flannery every single week for over a year with notes like, "I'd harvest coffee beans for five minutes with you."

Then there was the woman who snuck into their headquarters mailroom and worked for ten whole days before anyone thought to ask who she was. She thought her stealth initiative would impress Suzy. That one was successful, sort of. She was hired but to work in the mailroom. Not in marketing as she'd hoped.

But Alice worked at an O'Flannery firm already, and she was possibly a soon-to-be CFO.

Theodore's deep, resonant laughter reached her ears again.

But, shit, he worked there, too.

Concentrate on yourself. There was plenty to occupy her mind, including what was just outside her office door.

She studied the people milling about the cattle pen. Edison employees long ago renamed the maze of cubicles, often called a bullpen, to that more appropriate name. It fit the dirty gray fabric half-walls and lack of privacy. "It's where all creativity goes to wither and die," Patty once lamented.

Alice couldn't disagree.

Corrine, a junior sales assistant, and Tricia, who stood huddled over some paperwork, were shaking their heads. Probably another memo from Roger demanding to know what Corrine's compensation contract stated in response to a request for a new cell phone or laptop for Corrine's new duties. Alice could handle it with two phone calls, but Roger had to bless the purchases first. He made people justify every dime like it was his own.

Harrison and two of the marketing and sales guys were standing around holding Styrofoam cups. They didn't look very happy. She needed to find out who was in danger of not meeting quota and calm his nerves. Make sure Harrison hadn't moved on to liquor. They had been running low on coffee, and no one had thought to get more last week because she usually handled it. She'd buy more today … and maybe some no-name teabags that a certain someone hated.

Don't think about him.

"For the love of God," a male voice cried from the copier room across the hallway. She'd start there. She had hours before the O'Flannerys arrived, and it'd take all of twenty minutes to pull what Roger wanted.

Patty exaggerated the love affair between Alice and Big Whale, which she'd dubbed the large copy machine. But Alice seemed to be the only one who could ever scroll through its display memo to see why it'd stopped working.

Those were all things the office manager, Blanche, used to handle. But she'd left the company six months ago, and Roger hadn't wanted to add to payroll yet. The man had severely underestimated how many things could go wrong in a day.

Alice did whatever it took to keep the place running. She wasn't sorry to order office supplies and fix minor tech issues if it meant it'd count toward something better down the road. Maybe it was paying off after all.

She rounded the corner and ran smack into Theodore's chest. His familiar scent surrounded her, and a sizzle ran through her veins. She could recognize her reaction to him now. Pure physical attraction. Chemistry. A biological reaction. None of which was like her. Not at all. Even if Theodore had turned out to be a sex god—so opposite of his goofy first-impression.

But then his hand grasped both of her biceps, and the frisson of electricity grew like she'd morphed into a lightning bug—on steroids.

"Good morning, Miss Crawford." His eyes bore down on her.

"Mr. Gaston the *Fourth*."

One side of his mouth inched up as his eyes sparkled with amusement. "Good weekend?" He also was still touching her.

"Unhand me," she hissed. Jeez, he was rubbing off on her fast. She sounded like a British lord about to demand a duel. But another second of him touching her might have her ruin yet another pair of panties.

Who was that woman she'd let herself become?

He let go and stuffed his hands in his pocket, but his smirk didn't drop one bit. "Cranky. Need me to send you some motivational messages?"

She gasped. "Don't you dare." Her eyes flicked around the room to make sure no one was listening or noticing. Of course, all the women were looking their way. "We're on company property now, remember?"

"Property. Yes." He nodded slowly. "I'm quite busy today, anyway, Miss Crawford. Lots of interviews." He winked and strode past her.

Corrine sidled her way into his path. "Ready?" Her smile

was threatening to split her face. She was sweet and very good at her job if her sales reports were any indication. Even with a laptop as old as the dawning of the internet. She'd be sure the woman got a new one by end of day, despite her fawning over Theodore.

Theodore gestured for Corrine to step into his temporary office, ostensibly for their interview. Alice wasn't worried about Corrine's obvious fascination with Theodore. Every woman in the place had that same besotted look on their face. Even the married ones—like Corrine.

It had to be his energy—positive, easy-going, and confident. Or maybe it was the way he listened to you like you were the only person in the entire world. That would make a nun drop her habit like it was on fire. It certainly had for her.

Theodore's smile stayed camped on his face as Corrine entered his office.

"It's National Shareholders Day. Let's make them proud," he told her right before he closed his office door.

See? Charm incarnate. Alice shook her head and headed to the copier room. Peter stood with his back to her, punching the copier's display with so much gusto Alice's heart hurt for the machine.

"Peter." Crossing her arms, she leaned against the door frame. "Need help?"

He rolled his eyes and heaved a sigh. "Oh, thank God. You're back."

It took less than five minutes to get Big Whale working. Less time to assure Tricia she'd handle Corrine's laptop problem. Talking Harrison off the ledge, the one whose low sales this month were putting him in danger, took longer. But she gave him a Coffee Monkey gift card she had stashed in her desk drawer and told him to walk it off—after fueling up. That got a smile out of him.

She ran Roger's reports, ordered Corrine's laptop—hang Roger's demand to approve it—checked the most recent online supply order and ran a dozen expense reports.

She rose from her desk only every fifteen minutes to glance at Theodore's office door across the cattle pen's labyrinth of short walls. Her restraint for not staring at his door all day deserved a medal. Even from there, she could hear the giddy buzz of female voices rising up every time one of his interviewees left and a new one entered his den-of-female-adoration.

As the day progressed, the fact that he seemed to only interview the office's females irked her. That she was *irked* made her even more irked, until she was one big ball of *super-irked* tension. Why was she suddenly jealous? It was ridiculous. She was being ridiculous.

The rise of jealousy inside only added to her growing disappointment in herself. She had one sweaty, sexy weekend with the guy, a promise of further exploration in five months—on National BAE Day—and a deal they'd be professional.

Then it went all south when they almost got caught. So, she did what she had to do, right?

Well, now, she had a project to start that had some meat on its bones—finally. She opened the files on all the technology assets Edison owned or leased.

As she worked, she still couldn't help herself as she continued to sneak peeks through the long glass window alongside Theodore's closed door where he and now Jenny sat. Alice had to make sure his desk was still between them. Theodore was leaning back in his office chair, smiling and laughing. He was enjoying himself. Probably turning Jenny on to National Adopt an Armadillo Day.

Maybe Alice and Theodore could go to lunch together. Talk. That was what professional colleagues did all the time.

Stop it.

His door cracked open, and she plunked back down into her seat. She'd almost been caught spying. His low rumble reached her ears. Jenny made a delighted sound. Then laughter from more voices. Alice couldn't help herself. She slowly rose, likely resembling a gopher emerging from its hole.

Theodore was surrounded. Tricia, Jenny, Corrine, and now Patty—who she really hoped was spying for Alice—circled him in the hallway. All female eyes were trained on his face.

Then, abruptly, Theodore's hand went to Tricia's back, and the two of them strode toward the elevator. Tricia turned, waved to the other women, and winked. There was a message in that wink. *I bagged me a Jamie, ladies.*

Given it was 12:15 p.m., they were probably headed out for lunch. That was better than Alice's idea, anyway. She and Theodore shouldn't be seen together anymore.

The elevator doors whooshed open, and she had a quick moment of relief. The Twins, Suzy and Samuel O'Flannery, stood there. They were talking about something with each other, but they stopped as soon as they saw Theodore and Tricia.

Samuel was the first one out, a huge grin lighting up his face. "Theo. My man."

"Hey, mate," Theodore answered, his smile growing impossibly larger.

The two gave each other manly back slap hugs. As soon as they separated, Theodore's blue eyes turned to Suzy. They sparkled with pure joy, and Theodore quickly shoved Samuel aside. The man laughed about being thrown off.

Theodore opened his arms. "Suzy, get over here."

The woman moved in so quickly that Tricia had no choice but to take three steps back. Suzy threw her arms around him, then pulled back and gave him a big kiss. Right on the lips. It wasn't a peck, either. One thing was clear. They knew each other well.

And once again, he'd kept vital information from her. He knew the owners of Edison—as in *Kiss A Ginger Day well*. The bastard. The man was rife with secrets.

11

Suzy leaned back, holding his biceps. "Still as handsome as ever, I see." She brushed one hand along his cheek.

Theodore waggled his eyebrows. "Still can't keep your hands off me, I see." Suzy O'Flannery never changed, not even in her mid-forties. She was an unconscionable flirt—the opposite of her dead serious brother.

"That's what you get for being so adorable."

One thing for sure, no one's ego was in danger around her. "When are you going to quit the tech world and run off with me so we can make genius babies?"

She dropped her hands and laughed. "If we do, call the Vatican because a medical miracle has occurred."

Samuel lifted his chin. "Okay, you two. Run off to the supply closet and make good on these threats, or let's get rolling to the conference room." He clasped Theo on the shoulder. "We've got business to discuss."

Theodore huffed. "Such a drill sergeant. And here I thought you were coming to drag me off to another sake bar."

"You'll never forgive me for that night, will you?"

"Never." Theodore smiled over at his mate. "It wasn't even Sake Day. October 1, before you ask."

Samuel's low laughter warmed something in him. He'd missed having friends around. Always on the road, and all that.

Theodore had been friends with Suzy and Samuel for over a decade. They were responsible for his entire career. He'd worked for one of their tech start-ups, and it was Samuel who suggested he go into management consulting—more like browbeat him into it. Theodore agreed one night over an unwise quantity of sake, and the next morning, hungover as hell, he was on a plane to another one of their companies to "assess the situation honestly." A career was born.

Samuel looked around. "Where's Roger?"

"Haven't seen him all day, though I'm sure he's here somewhere." Theodore couldn't care less where Roger was. One thing he'd learned during the five or six interviews that morning, Roger wasn't popular at Edison Tech, and for good reason.

"Oh, he is. We just had a meeting." Alice had sidled up to them. She offered Suzy a huge smile. "Hi, I'm Alice Crawford. I wanted to introduce myself before you get mobbed by everyone else who wants to say hello." She held out her hand.

Suzy cocked her head and returned the handshake. "Alice. Nice to meet you. Our new CFO, right?"

Alice blinked. "Um, not yet."

Suzy's forehead furrowed. "Hmm. I see we do have a lot to catch up on here." She glanced at her brother, who was quite frankly studying Alice a little too hard. Theo recognized the look in his eyes. *Suspicion.*

He knew Samuel enough to know it wasn't interest. While Alice was a beautiful woman, Samuel would never act on any romantic inclination toward anyone at one of his companies. His one personal rule was never shag anyone at the office, which Theodore had spectacularly broken himself. Office romance wasn't legally forbidden, but Samuel certainly frowned upon it. Yet another reason to finally make good on his and Alice's deal to avoid one another for a bit. At least until he could sort through whatever the hell happened yesterday. One minute, they were enjoying each other. The next? He was a *mistake*. Hadn't Beatrice used almost the same word around being involved with him?

Samuel finally spoke up. "Well, if you see Roger, ask him to join us?"

Alice nodded once, then peered over at Theodore. Her smile dropped like a stone. Yeah, he was still in the faux pas column.

In the conference room, Samuel shed his jacket and threw it over a chair. "So, how's Edison so far?"

Suzy waved her hand as they all took seats at the long table. "He's been here for one weekend, Sam."

"And knowing Theo, he's already done a dozen interviews. Am I right, Theo?"

"Six. Actually seven." He'd count Alice and their time together as an interview.

Samuel's brow furrowed. "And?"

"And there's more to uncover. Something is off."

Samuel tipped his chin. "No kidding. Marketing costs are through the roof. Barely keeping people on payroll despite a sound product. Any idea what's happening?"

Finances wasn't what he was alluding to. More like a veil of unhappiness covering almost every employee.

Suzy reached over and smacked his arm as only a brother and sister could do and still be considered professionals. "Sam. One weekend. Give Theodore a break."

"There they are." Roger's voice boomed into the room, a little too loud, a little too high-pitched.

It was strange Samuel didn't stand. He wasn't usually rude. Direct, but always polite. Theodore glanced between the two men, trying to catch what past scenario caused the obvious rift—other than the fact the Wonder Kid CEO Roger wasn't being so wonderful these days.

Plus, he was reeked of some god-awful cologne.

Suzy shook Roger's hand, a tight smile on her face. "Roger. I trust you were expecting us."

"Of course, of course. Just had an emergency to attend to." Roger quickly raised both hands. "Nothing that couldn't be handled."

A rap on the door frame broke the sudden tension in the room. Alice held out a folder to Roger and gulped a little. "I ran those numbers for you. You may want to take a look first."

Roger threw her a hard look, growing red in the face. Suzy and Samuel glanced at each other. Ah, the financial reports weren't good.

Alice began to back away when Suzy rose from the table and strode forward. "Alice, why don't you join us?" She gestured for her to take a seat. "You're our numbers person."

"I'm sure Alice has many things on her plate today ..." Roger began but let his words die when Samuel drew out a chair for Alice.

"I'd love to. Thank you, Ms. O'Flannery. Mr. O'Flannery." She nodded in Samuel's direction.

"Samuel, please." A rare smile formed on his face.

After they were all seated around the conference table, Samuel held out his hand for the folder. Roger pushed it slowly across the table.

Samuel and Suzy slowly went through the P&L statement and balance sheet. A few well-placed *hmms* by Samuel and a few more pointed questions by Suzy had Roger visibly sweating. There was no explanation for the sudden downturn. Alice gave direct answers when asked, which Suzy did more and more, given Roger's clear ineptitude at providing basic information. Theodore, however? Silence was golden during a legendary O'Flannery deep dive into anything related to numbers.

Roger stretched his neck. "New products take time to launch, to grab market share." That was all Roger could come up with. The problem was Samuel and Suzy launched a dozen products a year—and none had failed as miserably as Edison Tech's recent offering, a security software program that detected problems in AI, like copyright infringement.

The not-too-wonderkid-CEO cleared his throat. "You're risk takers. Surely, you understand." Roger couldn't seem to stop digging his own grave. Telling the O'Flannerys who they were was an epic mistake.

"Risk? That's your answer?" Suzy asked icily.

"Alice," Roger sniffed. "As the acting CFO, I'd like to have learned of some of this earlier." He raised his eyebrows.

The man had to be kidding. Blaming Alice? Plus, what was that acting CFO thing? The damned liar.

Alice stiffened, a sliver of anger lighting up her eyes. Good woman. *Don't let him cow you.*

Suzy put both her hands on the table. "As CEO, I'd expect *you* to have kept a closer eye on things. Roger, we have much to discuss, don't we? But first, we'd like to talk to Alice. Mind giving us the room?"

The man's nostrils flared, but he rose, giving his jacket a dramatic tug. After he left, Suzy smiled over at Alice. "Does he do that often?"

Alice blinked as if she didn't understand the question.

"Yes," Theodore stated. "And not just on National Be a Dick Day." He was over being silent. Blaming Alice for Roger's incompetence had crossed a serious line.

Suzy raised one eyebrow. "Date?"

"October 19."

"You still got it. I suppose it's different from National Big Dick Day."

Theodore scratched his chin. "I've not measured the man, but—"

"Theodore." Samuel grimaced and held up his hand. "Maintain some decorum, you two. Alice will believe we're heathens."

"Roger could definitely celebrate," Alice blurted out. All eyes turned to her.

Suzy sat back in her chair, clearly amused. "Which one? Be a dick or big dick?"

She sat forward, her eyes clearing of whatever anger she'd felt. Ice had formed there. "Be a Dick Day. Sometimes. I wouldn't know about the … other. Thank God. I mean, there is no way. Nope."

Suzy's eyes sharpened, and, in a rare show of humor, Samuel laughed, scratching his chin. "Alice, could you run some other numbers for us? Help us uncover what's really happening here? Under double overtime, of course."

She visibly brightened. "Sure. What do you need?"

"The last five years, year-over-year marketing costs, a QoE report. Quality of Earnings, you know how?"

Theodore glanced at her. "You'll find Alice knows quite a bit—and about what happens here. And she's quite popular."

Oddly, her smile dropped at his compliment.

"I can see why," Samuel said. "Not many people are willing to step up and tell the truth, especially when it's not positive."

"Tell the Truth Day. July 7," Theodore said. "But you'll find Alice does that every day. So, when she said she wouldn't know about Big Dick Day, you can count on it."

Alice threw him a *shut-up already* look. "Of course, I

don't," she gritted out. "And yes, I can work on a QoE. Happy to."

Why was she upset? He was only trying to help her. Suzy, in particular, could sniff out an unflattering past like a drug detection dog, and Alice *had* revealed to him she'd gotten together with Roger outside the office. Times he'd clearly thought were dates.

Suzy stood. "Alice, while the men continue to mansplain all manners of trivia, how about you and I go over things. Without Roger. I found his answers lacking."

"That's not all he's lacking," Theodore muttered under his breath. He'd never understand what Roger gained from treating Alice so poorly. Something was amiss there.

In the doorway, Suzy turned to Alice. "Give me twenty minutes? I want to take a look around."

Suzy didn't look. She assessed, gathered evidence. She would engage in small talk with other employees, which she'd turn in her favor as expertly as a prosecutor. In under five minutes, she could ferret out a person's greatest secret, and they wouldn't even have known they'd revealed anything. Theodore had seen her work that magic a dozen times.

Roger was in so much trouble. Theodore wasn't sorry for him.

Samuel yawned. "I need coffee. Point me toward it?"

Alice pointed down the hallway. "Kitchen is that way, but our supply is pretty low. I was going to order more today. Have a favorite? I can be sure to have it delivered asap."

"Kona. Hawaiian."

"Consider it done."

"Thanks, Alice." Samuel was eyeing Alice too closely. Admiration for her people pleasing, perhaps? Or something else?

"I'll take you to Coffee Monkey," Theodore interjected. "Down the street."

He sliced his gaze Theodore's way. "I can get myself there. Wouldn't want to rip you from your admirers."

He glanced over his shoulder. Two women hovered nearby. Shit, he was late for an interview with ... someone. He couldn't recall her name. Come to think of it, there were a lot of women at Edison. He'd consider it progressive, except he was beginning to see a disturbing pattern around Roger's hiring habits. Half of the people at Edison were new. Their staff turnover was abysmally high.

He turned back to Samuel. "No admirers. Work."

"Speaking of which, why don't I grab my laptop, so I have everything at my fingertips. Then, Suzy, join you in the conference room?"

Suzy smiled. "Perfect."

Alice gave a little half wave and scooted away.

Suzy's gaze followed Alice's retreat. "You *do* have an admirer, don't you?" She smirked up at him. "I haven't seen someone try to act that normal around you that hard since Flanapp Tech." Ah, her tech baby that went belly up. No fault of her own. It was thanks to one of the programmers who'd launched a ransomware attack on the company. Ransom he took the liberty to pay—to himself. The man was serving back-to-back sentences in some jail in Illinois, last he'd heard.

"No admirers I'm aware of. Besides, you two probably intimidated Alice."

"She doesn't seem easily intimidated. I like her," Suzy said definitively. "If she isn't CFO by the end of the day, we'd be fools."

"She's competent." A sad word to replace the truth of the women's obvious skills.

"And pretty," Suzy said.

The interrogation had begun. Time to deflect. "Oh? I hadn't noticed."

Samuel chuffed. "No trysts at the office, right?" He pointed and headed to the elevator, ostensibly to get his chosen coffee. The man had a serious addiction—and very specific tastes.

While Suzy went sleuthing and Samuel got caffeinated, Theodore would find Alice. He strode through the nearly empty cubicle farm. The workers fled like a flock of starlings at lunchtime as if they couldn't wait to get away.

He found her in the copy room. He stood in the doorway far too long, watched her shuffle papers back and forth on the table.

When he cleared his throat, she jumped backward. A little yip left her throat, and her hand flew to her chest. "Theodore."

"Alice." He closed the door behind him. Ah, a lock he'd never noticed before. He used it. When he turned to face her, she stood with arms crossed, eyes afire.

He stuffed his hands in his trousers and leaned back against the door. "What's wrong?"

"What was that?" She jerked her hand toward the bullpen.

"Our meeting?" It was as good a guess as any. "Where Roger called you acting CFO?"

"No. I mean all that ... flirting. In front of *them*." She was shout-whispering, which was silly given they were alone. In a locked room.

He strode forward and she backed up. Afraid to get close? "Your eyes really sparkle when you're annoyed."

"I don't *sparkle* at work."

"Oh, yes, you do. Though, technically, National Sparkle Day is February 27." One more step toward her. One big step backward from her. He sighed heavily.

"Enough of the days!" Her hands slapped her thighs, and her hazel eyes fired anew.

"It's harmless fun."

"Is that all this is to you? Fun?"

He knew where she was headed. "You have nothing to worry about." He honestly couldn't imagine anyone but her. "And about Samuel and Suzy—"

"Could have thought I'm not serious."

"Relax. They're pros. And besides, you're the one who brought up Roger's … *fit* into it."

"Hardly. You did." She poked him in the chest. "And for the record, Roger threw me under the bus in that meeting."

"I know. I was there, remember?" His chest tightened. Roger wasn't only an unpopular person at Edison, he also was a weak one. CEOs didn't throw shade on employees publicly—at least not the good ones.

She chewed on one side of her fingernail. "And here I thought he was finally considering me for that promotion. Turns out he just wants me for more work."

"What?"

"He came to me this morning with more projects and said I was still in the running for CFO."

"I'd say you're more than in the running. Suzy liked what you said about Roger." He grinned down at her and leaned forward. "She likes *you*. And she doesn't like most people."

That got her attention. She straightened to her full height. "She does? How do you know?" Her eyes narrowed. God, she was a complicated woman.

"We've been friends for a while."

"Which you never told me, by the way." Her finger jabbed him in the chest again.

He grabbed it, and her breath hitched. His cock woke up. Their chemistry thing was damned inconvenient. One touch, one little suck of breath between her lips, and he was ready to push her over that monstrosity of a copier, yank down her panties, and …

"Let go. Please." Her voice held a plea. She knew how dangerous they were together. Like two sticks of dynamite near a bonfire—a fire they started every time they got near one another.

He dropped his hold on her hand. But then she bit her bottom lip, and his rather problematic arousal blew up. His zipper began to strain. "Alice."

"Theodore."

They stood there, staring at one another. Inextricably, a laugh burst out of them both.

"Oh, ffyc me." He pinched the bridge of his nose. "You have a meeting with Suzy. I have an interview I'm late for."

"Yeah, I guess us getting it on against the copier isn't a good idea."

He stilled. "I thought I was a mistake."

"No. Not a mistake. Getting caught was."

Ridiculous relief coursed through his veins. "Well, I'm glad we cleared that up. So, let's not get caught. Because we're amazing together."

She rolled her eyes as if he were the idiot of the century. Of course, she did. They were long past dismissing their attraction to one another. Resisting it, however, proved to be the challenge.

"We can talk about that later. I have to get back to work," she said. "Besides, you have at least three women waiting for you."

"Alice." She needed to stop overthinking things. But what could he say? Defending himself wouldn't make a difference. It certainly hadn't with Beatrice, who always accused him of some romantic travel tryst. But cheating wasn't part of his make-up. "Don't be angry with me."

"I'm not. Not really. More mad at myself."

He lifted his hand to tuck a piece of hair behind her ear, but she backed up.

"Tell me you weren't withholding your friendship with the O'Flannerys from me?" she said with a lilt.

"I work for them. Of course, I know them. They own Edison, and you know that. Didn't think I had to bring it up."

"Weak, but I'll give you a pass on it." She drew closer to him and ran her hand down his tie. "Thanks for … defending me in there."

He finally got to run his fingers through her hair. "Always. You deserve it." She pressed her cheek into the palm of his hand.

No one could ever call Theodore hesitant in shying away from the obvious truth. Staying away from her would prove … difficult. His ability to stay focused weakened, his body hummed with her awareness whenever she was around. He couldn't *not* touch her when they were this close. At least that was what he'd tell himself later as to why he bent his head down and captured her lips with his. It was as if he were a drug addict. He was addicted to her taste. He had to have a hit. Just one.

But then her lips parted, and his tongue found its way between them to that sweet, sweet taste of Alice.

One kiss, his ass. He deepened their mouth lock, and a loud thud of their bodies sounded as her back hit the copier. He had her up against the thing and was grinding his stone-hard erection between her legs within seconds because, God love the woman, she opened them to him immediately.

A small whimper left her throat. The urge to hoist her up on to the giant copier exploded—just as the machine let out a long hiss and bang.

He jumped backward as if his brain finally re-engaged. The thing was alive?

Alice panted. "Big Whale is—"

"In love with you. I heard. Registering his protest?"

She laughed, then sobered, running her hands down the front of her jacket. "Or saving us from doing something foolish." Her finger circled in the air. "Work, remember?"

He leaned down and whispered in her ear. "You busy tonight?"

"It's going to be a late night. Suzy wants my help."

"But later?"

"What did you have in mind?"

He pulled out his cell phone and handed it to her. "Give me a call."

"What?"

"I don't have your number. Call yourself."

She took it and called her own cell. "Okay. Connected. Now, what? Going to call me later and ask me on a date?"

He repocketed his mobile and slowly shook his head. "Something far better."

"Hey, how long you going to be?" a voice shouted on the other side of the door. "I got a deadline here."

He glanced at the door, then leaned toward her. "You ever had text sex, Miss Crawford?"

She swallowed. "Not any good sexting," she whispered back.

"Challenge accepted." He picked up her hand, kissed it, and unlocked the door. "Got to respect those deadlines."

Peter, a junior marketing associate, burst in. "Please tell me it's working."

"It's working all right." He'd make sure of it.

Alice couldn't dismiss them any longer. Their chemistry? It moved from mere attraction to something real. They couldn't stay away from one another, and he'd prove to her they didn't even need to be in the same room to combust in the best way possible.

12

———

Theodore proved he was a man of his word. As soon as she got home, bleary-eyed from staring at spreadsheets for hours, her phone pinged.

Alice stared at her phone screen.

<<In the words of Taylor Swift, are you ready for it? >>

God, please don't let him be quoting her. Taylor rocked, but Alice wanted hardcore *Outlander* throw-me-on-the-bank-of-the-nearest-loch-and-shed-your-kilt sexting, not love song lyrics.

She'd fielded Suzy's questions over Chinese take-out cartons for two hours. She loved her time with the woman —*loved* it. But she could barely keep up. It was only when she couldn't stifle a single yawn that Suzy suggested they start fresh in the morning.

There also was the matter of every time her phone vibrated, Theodore's offer of text sex came rushing back to her. She would have to stash extra panties in her desk drawer for as long as Theodore was working at Edison.

<<Define "it">> She'd get the terms right off the bat.

<<Worshipping from a respectable distance. Do you know the first order of business?>>

<<Asking me what I'm wearing>>

<<Love, I'd never be that pedestrian. Clothes are the last thing on my mind.>>

Hers, too. She jogged to her bedroom, threw the phone so hard it bounced off the mattress to the floor, and yanked off her coat. Within seconds, the rest of her clothes joined it on the floor. Theodore seemed to make her do that—rip her clothes off her like a wild animal, as he'd said.

Another cheery chime went off on her now-abandoned phone. She grabbed it from the floor.

<<Besides, I know you're naked.>>

She gasped, glanced around. As if she'd find him behind the curtains? <<How do you know>>

<<Even from here, I can scent your skin.>>

Oh, feral. A deep thudding pulsed between her legs. She didn't have a lot of experience in sexting, but he clearly knew what he was doing. Proper punctuation and everything. But, of course, he'd be a sexting god. Look at how good he was at the actual deed.

What could she say that would be scintillating? A deep buzzing in her ears kept her from coming up with anything. She wanted to match his enthusiasm, but her skills were in analyzing numbers, not words that might make him go full flagpole. And she really, really wanted him at full mast.

More dots started to float across her screen. She stared at them as if they were the Holy Grail.

<<Location is first. It's International Bathtub Day. Give you any ideas?>>

<<Into water sports?>>

<<If it involves you nude, I'm into anything.>>

Hmmm, sexting in the tub. Not a bad idea. She could use some unwinding.

Her phone pinged again. <<**Don't leave me standing here in my birthday suit too long, Alice. Mrs. Peterson next door loves to peek at my goods through my curtains.**>>

He knew his neighbors already? Of course, he did.

She was moving to her bathroom before she even finished reading the message. She furiously typed. <<**You're off limits to Mrs. Peterson. Your goods are mine**>> She didn't know where she got the cajónes to write that. But no one could ever accuse her of not being one hundred percent into whatever job was at hand.

<<**Meet your spectacular breasts and ass in the tub.**>>

Who was she to argue? Heat bathed her from head to toe anyway.

A quick glance at her tub cooled her instantly. Needed cleaning. Nothing would get you examining a tub's surface faster than having to fill it with hot water and sink your naked body into it to have text sex with a hot ginger who believed you had a spectacular ass and breasts.

Her phone pinged again. <<**Unless you'd rather celebrate Yodel for Your Neighbors Day.**>>

If he thought he could get out of what he'd started, he had another thing coming. <<**Does yodeling turn you on?**>> *Please type no.*

<<**Only if we do it together, naked, in the tub.**>>

<<**Give me a minute. I like my water hot**>>

<<**Like your men.**>>

His ego certainly was intact. <<**one sec**>>

She opened the cabinet under the sink and pulled out her cleaning supplies—gloves, scrubber, bleach. With a loud slap, she had her gloves on in a second.

Her screen lit up again from a text from him. <<**Gotta clean it first, eh?**>>

Damn him. If he'd hidden a camera, she'd sue *his* very fine ass. She yanked off the gloves.

<<**I'll have you know, Theodore Gaston the Fourth I am assessing how much water I should use. I mean if there's going to be water sloshing around or not**>> Liar, liar, rubber gloves on fire.

<<**Maximum sloshing.**>>

Game on.

But first, a clean tub was necessary. She'd never attacked a job so fast, making big circles with the cleaner and a touch of bleach. She might be in the tub for a while.

Within minutes, her body was slick with water that had splashed across her skin. It wasn't her smartest idea to be doing it naked. Bleach burned. But the way her breasts pressed against the cold tub edge, she found it oddly refreshing. When did she ever hang out nude? How about never?

Another ping sounded and echoed off the bathroom tile. <<**Two minutes and the water will cover your favorite part of me.**>> Didn't all men say their penis was their favorite?

<<**Your photographic memory?**>>

<<**Need a picture to remember?**>>

Oh, God, a dick pick? No, thanks. <<**I'd rather it be in person**>>

He didn't answer that one. Probably because he was enjoying his *favorite part*.

She quickly rinsed off the tub, soaking her arms, chest, thighs, and floor, but who cared? She was about to get wet. And with any luck, wet *everywhere*. She abandoned her gloves and began to fill the tub.

She typed as she watched the water rise—too slowly. <<**And what is my favorite part doing now?**>>

<<**Drowning. Care to launch a rescue?**>>

<<**Need a little mouth to mouth?**>>

<<He's waking up at your offer. But you should. In case he needs greater resuscitating.>>

She swallowed, which did little to keep her mouth from craving him—and his favorite part. Many women declared they hated oral sex—giving it, not receiving it. Not her. She loved it all.

Plus, she really did love a man who could spell.

She dipped her foot into the water and hissed. Too hot. But she had a rescue to start. She cranked the cold to even out the temperature and managed to lower herself to the two inches of water that pooled around her. It wasn't the most graceful move, given she had to hold on to her phone at the same time.

Once settled, she returned her attention to her screen. Typing was challenging with just her thumb, but a certain man part needed her. **<<Now are YOU ready for it?>>**

The screen lit up again with another of Theodore's messages. **<<How's that glorious bottom feeling?>>**

<<Wet>>

<<Enjoying the heat?>>

A rush of how his cock felt inside her—hot, long, full—cascaded into her mind. **<<I'd enjoy it more if something hot was inside me>>** That message wasn't half bad. Maybe he was wearing off on her.

<<Now you've done it. He's fully alive. Touch yourself.>>

Going straight to it. Her fingers slipped between her legs, and a deep sigh rumbled up from her chest and out her lips.

<<Small circles, love.>>

<<Bossy>> Her thumb began to ache from the awkward texting. So did another part of her anatomy.

<<If you'd like.>>

<<I lidg>> Shit, she couldn't do it one handed.

<<Lidg's not my favorite move.>>

Making fun of her? <<**You try texting one handed**>> She should switch to voice, but the stupid AI woman was always getting her words wrong.

<<**I am.**>>

Oh. He was handling himself. At least she imagined so. <<**Long strokes or short?**>>

<<**Both. How's the sloshing?**>>

The water had risen at that point but wasn't threatening to slosh anywhere—yet. <<**Tub is holding**>>

<<**Can't say the same.**>>

The mental picture of him fisting himself, hard and fast, sped her own hand up. <<**How hard?**>> She somehow managed to type words.

<<**Steel. Imagining myself inside you right now is fucking fantastic.**>>

She dipped one finger inside herself. Imagined him there. <<**Clenching down on you hard**>>

<<**You want me to fuck you harder, don't you?**>>

Theodore had a sailor mouth, er, texting finger. Her clit began to throb, and her legs ached to spread even farther apart than the tub allowed. <<**Yes**>> She reached over and shut off the water. Then she swung one leg over the edge and pushed her finger inside herself, deeper. The move was a poor substitute for Theodore.

<<**I'd also make you get on all fours so I could thrust inside you.**>>

The man turned downright feral during sex. Her body was so on board with it.

Her forehead pricked from the heated water, and her mouth fell open as a flood of sensation cascaded down her legs. She'd give anything to have a second set of hands. She wanted to touch herself—everywhere—imagining it was Theodore doing exactly what he wrote.

<<**More**>> She then dropped her phone to the bathroom rug and sped up her hand.

Somewhere along the way, all her inhibitions had fled. As if she could hang on to them with Theodore around. He brought things out in her she didn't know she had.

Her phone began to ping like crazy. The little chirping sounds bounced off the tile and mixed with the water splashes. Theodore was texting her like a man possessed. She channeled every bit of that thought into imagining him thrusting into her fast and hard.

Her climax went on and on, and she milked it for a long minute.

It took a while to reclaim her breath, open her eyes. Water had definitely breached the side of the tub. She wiped her hand on a nearby towel and picked up her phone.

Several text threads began to compete with each other.

Theodore's came in first. <<**Fucking you ... hard.**>>

Patty's text popped up next. <<**Alice! Red alert. The office was robbed.**>>

<<**Jesus, you're tight. Hot. Wet.**>>

Theodore, then Patty. Then Patty again until Alice grew dizzy.

<<**Roger is losing it. Tricia called. Call me?**>>

<<**Pumping into you deeper now.**>>

<<**Alice, where are you? Tried calling. Is your phone on silent again?**>>

<<**Comig so hardd. wrjht.**>>

Her mind didn't know where to go first. Thoughts buzzed around her head like a bumble bee.

Theodore masturbating in the tub to images of her.

The office being broken into.

Theodore getting off *so hard* he mistyped.

The fact that she'd unwisely set her phone to silence everything but her text messages when meeting with Suzy.

Theodore—*hot, hot* Theodore.

Roger losing it.

Theodore.

Finally, her phone stopped making any noise at all. An endless minute stretched out. What was important at that very second? She texted Theodore back. <<**Me too**>> Then dialed Patty's number.

13

—————

Mondays were usually a zoo. Add a burglary and Alice didn't know what she would encounter.

The night before, Tricia had texted to say the building's alarm went off at 10:38 p.m. The cameras caught a guy in a hooded sweatshirt and jeans running through the parking lot, his backpack bumping on his back. He held something under his arm—the petty cash box, which Alice had stored in her locked desk drawer.

Police took fingerprints. Stolen items were cataloged. The thief had snatched really odd things: Roger's fountain pen, a crystal paperweight, the Keurig machine, and all the K-cups, including the disgusting blueberry cobbler coffee that only Tricia liked. Alice would have willingly given the guy those if he'd only left the French roast and Samuel's special Kona blend. Whoever the thief was, he was about to be the most hated human at Edison Tech. No caffeine at Edison could start a war.

As soon as Alice and Patty stepped off the elevator, they both scanned the office. It was empty, but it didn't look any different from yesterday, except for the poor fig tree by the elevator doors, now on its side, a scattering of dirt over the gray carpet.

The air felt different, though. A hush hung in the air like smoke. Being burgled *would* change the mood, but the quiet was oppressive.

"Where is everyone?" she whispered to Patty, who she'd picked up again that morning because her car was in the shop. "You know Roger didn't give anyone the day off." He never did.

Patty shrugged. "Maybe Harrison brought the good pastries from the German deli?"

That would send anyone running to their tiny kitchen, turning it into the Thunderdome, especially because there'd be no coffee unless someone ran out for it. She couldn't imagine the whole office would be at the Coffee Monkey café down the street at once.

Or maybe everyone was in one of Roger's sudden all-staff meetings.

That thought must have dawned on both her and Patty at the same time. They slowly blinked at one another. Without another word, they scooted toward the conference room. Sure enough, Roger was giving one of his morning "prep talks." The fact that he used the wrong word for "pep talk" was apropos because there was nothing motivating about his impromptu gatherings.

The room was fairly crowded; though the O'Flannerys were conspicuously missing. Other than pastries from the German deli, nothing else brought workers to a meeting faster than getting all the juicy details of something like an office burglary.

Theodore sat back, his ankle on his knee, rocking back and forth in his chair, listening intently to Roger. Tricia sat next to Theodore, her gaze roaming Theodore from head to foot.

His penetrating blue eyes flicked up to Alice once, then returned to Roger. Not even giving her a second glance.

She'd called him right after she got the downlow from Patty. Alice let him in on what happened, and he seemed oddly nonplussed about the whole matter. They didn't talk long. Probably for the best because it was time to work, not imagine filthy sexual things that still crowded her mind.

She tried hard to concentrate on Roger's talk instead of remembering Theodore's words last night. *Imagining myself inside you right now is fucking fantastic.*

Her thighs squeezed together as if that would stem her rising lust just from being near him again.

Alice tried hard to concentrate on Roger's voice. Instead, the expected words from him floated into one ear and out the other. *We're handling things with the authorities. If anything seems suspicious, like you're missing anything, anything at all, report it to me. I'm really going to miss that fountain pen.*

Low chuckles filled the room at his attempt at humor.

Her mind fixated on trying to remember how much money was in the stolen petty cash box and when the Twins might show up. They'd been warned they were coming again. In fact, she was surprised Roger wasn't talking about *that*.

Roger clapped his hands together and rubbed them. "All right, everyone back to work. We've got a bottom line to watch." He then proceeded to watch Janie's perky little bottom sway its way to the door. Yep. She'd been ID'd to be his Miss January, all right. She made a mental note: Check in on Janie. Make sure she was okay with Roger's attention.

"What'd we miss?" Patty asked Harrison as soon as he got closer.

Alice didn't have time to wait for his answer because Roger was next to her in seconds. "Alice? My office, please?"

Once inside Roger's office, he gently closed the door behind them. "You were late again."

Jesus. "I was here until nine last night. With Suzy."

Surprise flashed across his eyes. He didn't know. Then again, when had he ever stayed past 5:30 p.m.?

He cleared his throat. "Well, you heard about the break-in. The petty cash box was in your office."

"Locked," she reminded him.

"Of course. Not a big deal. A few hundred dollars—"

"Thousands." She didn't know the exact amount, but it was way more than a few hundred bucks.

He stilled and blinked at her. Another surprise to him?

It was her turn to clear her throat. "Six thousand four hundred on my last count." She hadn't paid much attention to it lately. "You'd asked me to keep about ten grand on hand, so—"

"I did, did I?" His tone was rather accusatory. "I don't remember that."

How could he forget? He was always dipping into the fund. "You said for emergencies. Suddenly needing a new printer or—"

"All right. All right." He glanced at his watch. It looked new. What happened to the Rolex? Though that one looked equally expensive. "Suzy and Samuel will be here soon. Now, we need a united front on this thing."

He couldn't be serious. They certainly weren't united yesterday. "On?"

"Let's say the petty cash was taken. But it was a minor amount."

"Oo-kay." It wasn't minor. Most businesses kept less than a thousand on hand, but Roger was in love with cash, so she'd pushed his odd request out of her mind long ago. She had more pressing matters to attend to.

"And about that asset management plan, I'm afraid I'll have to move that up on you."

"You'll have it on your desk by end of day."

His chin jutted backward. "That soon?"

"Suzy gave me a template, and—"

"You and Suzy are getting awfully chummy. Theodore, too, I noticed."

"Yes, Suzy has been great," she agreed, even though one solo meeting with the woman would hardly constitute best pals. But she would soak up every word Suzy O'Flannery said while she spent time with her. As for Theodore, she wouldn't go there with him.

"I care about your career. Just be careful. Wouldn't want you to—"

"Get ahead of my skis?"

He leaned down. "Get played."

Before she could respond, the door cracked open and a female voice asked, "How much was taken?"

Alice nearly jumped out of her skin. Suzy O'Flannery stood in her doorway. Her mouth was set in a hard line, and her eyes lasered in on Roger.

Roger, who also had been startled, recovered well. "Not much in the way of petty cash, if that's what you're asking. A few trinkets. Likely a street kid, wanting money for drugs."

"Hmmm, you could be right. Though to go to all the trouble of going up to the eighteenth floor?" She glanced around behind her. "To this office? No other tenants were burgled?"

"I'm not certain," he said cautiously.

Another long *hmm* came out of Suzy. "Alice, what say you and I continue where we left off last night. Roger, Samuel is looking for you."

So much fear filled Roger's face, Alice was embarrassed for him. But her sympathy for him had a definite limit. He once again made Alice question where the hell she stood at the company. She could bring it up with Suzy, but then she might look desperate. Then again, she wasn't about to go down for Roger's mismanagement. She'd figure out how to share the real amount of the petty cash to Suzy somehow.

As for Roger bringing up Theodore, she had nothing to be ashamed of. They were merely exploring, and she could separate work from pleasure. No problem.

14

Alice rubbed the spot between her eyes and tried to focus on the document she'd been reading—or, in her case, re-reading for the third time to try to make sense of the words on the paper.

Yet another burst of laughter filled the air. It took a Herculean effort not to glance up to see who Theodore was enchanting today in his office. His deep baritone rumbled something, and like clockwork a slight throb grew between her thighs.

Jesus. She'd never taken herself as someone who got so wrapped up in a guy that the mere sound of his voice turned her into a tuning fork. Perhaps she'd been hypnotized by his romantic Welsh accent and hand skills, something she couldn't stop thinking about.

Alice should move her desk. That way she couldn't hear him or see him—and his growing harem—from across the cattle pen. In. Out. In. Out. For three days, Edison Tech employees paraded into his office. Sometimes more than once. Smiling. Laughing. Relaxed—a state she hadn't felt in days.

She and Theodore had hardly gotten any time together, though he always stopped in to see her a few times a day, and they'd had another sexting session two evenings ago. So unsatisfying. There was nothing like the real thing.

Andy from R&D rushed into her view. "Hey, Alice, got a second?"

She was fresh out of them, but … "Sure. What's up?"

"Something's wrong with my direct deposit. Bank put a hold on it for some reason."

That didn't sound right. "Let me call them. See what's up."

It had to be a glitch—another one to add to the every-growing pile of recent breakdowns.

The other day, the internet went down for two hours, which sent everyone into a tizzy. Thirty minutes with tech support solved it. Two older laptops died on two of the sales guys. That was meltdown-worthy because they didn't keep any computers in reserve. Roger hadn't wanted to spend the money.

The only part of Alice's job that was working was her meetings with Suzy. She had to pinch herself that *the* Suzy O'Flannery was taking such an interest in her, explaining certain things without making her feel like a complete idiot. Like how a nontraded real estate investment trust was struc-tured and other complex financial instruments Alice had been trying to learn.

They'd often get interrupted because some emergency would crop up. Like they were getting low on K-cups of everyone's new favorite Hawaiian Kona coffee. Now that Alice had replenished the supply with Samuel's chosen coffee, the entire office had upgraded their idea of what constituted good java.

Theodore's door cracked open. Janie walked backward out of it as if she didn't want to rip her gaze from his strong jaw or his I'll-devour-you grin.

It was a familiar scene.

Theodore leaned against the door jamb, casting his beautiful eyes down on Janie. Her light laughter followed.

She tried to not eavesdrop on them, but her ears seemed attuned to his voice.

Yesterday, she'd overheard him and Tricia talking outside the kitchen area.

Oh, Theodore, that tea you recommended? Fabulous. Thank you so much.

His low rumble murmured. *Always a pleasure. Never a chore.*

He'd used that line on her.

Then, when Georgia, a junior marketing assistant, had asked him for places to visit in London—a trip she suddenly "felt compelled to plan," he'd typed a long list into her phone. Alice watched him spend ten minutes tapping away.

That wasn't all. Two women met with him at once earlier that day. They kept darting glances at each other as if to mentally telepathize *Can you believe it? We're here ... with Theodore!* They laughed so much at that meeting, Alice knew hearts were melting for him. And he basked in all the adoration.

Maybe he was a sex addict. They needed a lot of attention from the opposite sex, right? Except he never once crossed the line into wholly inappropriate talk at work. At least not from what she could hear.

Who was she to judge anyway? Her imagination, for one, was no better. It was his hands. She kept thinking about them—on her. She knew he wasn't taking any of those girls home but still...

To manage her overactive imagination, she'd started a spreadsheet to keep track of all the little things she was growing irritated with to try to sort through them later and make sure she wasn't overreacting or losing her mind. It was a sort of pro and con list, all neatly organized.

In the pro list, she'd listed "always says hello in the morning and stops by at least two times during the day." Granted, his voice maintained a neutral business tone, but a greeting was a greeting.

In the con list was "evokes too many made-up holidays" and "displays a shocking level of ingratitude." That last one earned him bold text. He did not at all appreciate the tea pods she ordered for the Keurig. She sprung for the Twinings, too. She left a box on his desk, only to find them in Tricia's hands in the kitchen.

Theodore's chuckle from down the hallway shook her out of her spiral. She turned away to go back to her desk. But before she could sit, Harrison's frame filled her doorway. Angst lined his face. "She's down again."

For the love of… "Again? I swear I don't know what you do to Big Whale."

"That copier has a vendetta against me."

She followed him to the copier room. Inside, Theodore stared down at a temp they'd hired that morning to help with some database input. Maven, Mabel, May-something?

He had his arms crossed and was rocking back on his heels as he said, "I swear. It's all true."

She stared up at him like stars shot out of his eyes.

"Spreading rumors about how handsome I am, again?" Harrison interjected.

Theodore slapped him on the shoulder. "That would be you bragging about my brilliant mind."

Harrison chuckled and might have blushed a little. *Jesus.* The love-fest never ended.

The temp worker—Mary, maybe?—had a killer smile. It was aimed firmly at Theodore, of course. "More like how if a

Buckingham Palace guard smiles, it's considered a breach of their duty." She sighed. "So, have you ever been inside?"

Theodore leaned down toward her. "I can safely say I've never been granted an audience, but one can dream, May Lynn."

So close on the name …

The woman tittered and slapped him on the arm. Her hand lingered a bit. "It must be so exciting to live in London. Your whole family lives there?"

"He's from Wales, not England," Alice said and strode over to the copier, whose dashboard was lit up like Times Square on New Year's Eve.

"Yes, true Welshman here," he said. "But I do live in London."

See? She knew nothing about the man. "How nice for you. A bachelor pad in every city."

May Lynn lowered her voice and aimed it right at Alice. "It's called a flat in the UK."

"I know." She stared down at the blinking screen. "You done with your project, May Lynn?"

"Not yet, but I'll get back to it," May Lynn said brightly. "Let me know if you need any help, Theodore. I'm here all day."

He dipped his chin. "Lovely to meet you."

"I love the way you talk." May Lynn finally scooted out.

Harrison grinned over at Theodore. "Maybe I should adopt a British accent."

Alice loved Theodore's accent, but that didn't stop her from an internal eye roll.

Harrison glanced over at Alice. "So, verdict?"

She punched the reset button. The display screen began blinking rapidly. *Fantastic.* "We may have to call the repair man. I haven't seen this before."

Harrison huffed. "Jerry over at Cis-com wants a paper

proposal sent over by end of day. And I got"—he pulled out his phone—"two calls and—"

"Leave it with me. I'll run out at lunch and have it back by one."

He sighed in relief. "You're a life saver, Alice."

He left her with Theodore, who oddly hadn't budged. "Your boyfriend giving you trouble, Miss Crawford?"

Alice tried hard to not look at Theodore. "Big Whale is not my boyfriend. More like my pain in the ass." She bent down toward the screen and whispered, "Forget I said that." She circled to the back of the copier. Maybe if she unplugged it, the thing would reset. That'd worked before.

He leaned against the machine. "You run errands for others a lot?"

"Why do you care?"

"What's got your knickers in a twist, love?"

"I'm not in a twist, Theodore." She knew she sounded *exactly* like her panties were tied in a bow cutting off her lady bits' circulation. The interruptions that day were getting out of hand.

She tried to pull out the plug, which was the size of a cell phone. It wasn't budging. "Just tired. It's been a busy day."

"Let me help." He reached for her.

"I got it."

His large hand curled around hers. Sparks flew up her arm, and she jumped. His hand, curled in a fist, pulled back.

"Industrial carpeting," she said.

His brows shot up. "What's that?"

"Static electricity. That's all it was." She reached over again and pulled the plug hard. It came loose.

"Sure, Alice. Whatever you say." Now, he sounded irritated.

"Happens all the time."

"That right?" He shoved his hand in his trouser pockets. "Doesn't happen all the time to me."

She got his meaning. "I'd say *it* happens to you every day."

"What are you talking about?" He scrubbed his hair, clearly exasperated.

"Oh, Theodore, that tea you recommended? Fabulous. Oh, Theodore, I love the way you talk." She batted her eyelashes at the ceiling.

He snorted through his nostrils. "You're jealous?"

"No. I'd very much like to not be bothered by any of this at all." That was the truth. She didn't want her attraction to him. The attention on Theodore was too consuming. "It's taking over my life."

"I'd say this place"—he waved his hand around the air—"has taken over your life. You work too much."

"And you? You seem to be the office comedian."

"People reveal a lot more when not stressed. What is going on with you? Really?" His brow furrowed, and he stepped forward.

She moved back, an automatic reaction. She'd been trying so hard to resist him. She needed space so she could *think,* not just physically react to him.

He strode to the door, flipped the secure sign, and shut the door. He turned to her. "Truth. What's wrong?"

"Please don't."

"Don't what?" He was getting dangerously close to her now. But it was when his hand reached out to grasp her arm and he slid his large palm down to her hand that the sparks turned into lightning. He gave her fingers a gentle squeeze, and she melted.

He arched an eyebrow in question. She forgot what she was protesting altogether because, again, *puddle.*

A knock sounded on the door. "Got her fixed? Deadline moved up." It was Harrison's booming voice. She didn't know whether she should thank him or be pissed. Theodore had definitely planned to kiss her. God, she'd wanted him to.

They were playing a dangerous game. Even being in the same office was too much, and she couldn't screw up. Not now.

"I have to go." She yanked open the door and scooted out of there fast, passing Harrison. "Not fixed," she said to him. Nothing seemed to be.

15

───────

Theodore rested his chin on his hand and watched Alice feed documents into a shredder inside her office door. Something was seriously wrong with her. He needed to talk to Suzy and Samuel and get them to lay off a bit with all the requests. Suzy was a drill sergeant, and Samuel didn't understand the word *rest*.

They were corporate through and through, ensuring their employees never caught up. Down time was wasted time to them.

Theodore was late to a meeting with Samuel to download his latest interview findings. Edison had a lot of employees— more than 150—and a definite pattern was emerging. No one was happy to be there.

He rose, stretching his back. A yawn came out of nowhere, practically splitting his jaw. He'd swing by and get some coffee before heading over to the conference room where Samuel was camped.

Roger and Janie, a petite blonde, were hovering around the coffee machine. Upon seeing Theodore, the man straightened. "Theodore," he said.

Janie stepped backward, averting her eyes as if she'd just gotten both hands, and maybe both feet, caught in Roger's cookie jar. "See you gentleman later." She scooted out.

Ah, Miss January, perhaps? She didn't mention anything like that earlier, but he knew all about Roger's office dalliances. It was Tricia who'd spilled the beans on that particular habit of Roger's. She'd taken great delight in sharing the guy's short-term office romances, which sounded more like a nineteen-year-old college student bar hopping. Roger's extracurricular activities was something Theodore would eventually have to share with Samuel, who would make the man immediately pack it in.

Perhaps Theodore's own guilt for hooking up with Alice had him hesitate. She certainly seemed to regret their time together by her behavior today.

Then again, her workaholic tendencies were starting to catch up with her. Dark circles had formed under her eyes, and her behavior was entirely too snappish.

Theodore cracked open a cabinet and retrieved a mug with gold letters emblazoned with Edison Tech on it. "Roger," he said.

"How are the interviews?" Roger took a sip of his coffee.

Theodore popped in a K-cup, not even looking at which one he chose. "Productive."

"We have good employees here."

"You do. By the way, what happened to the CFO? And the office manager? Did they quit, or were they let go?" He knew they'd quit, but he needed to hear Roger's version.

"Moved on to new opportunities. It happens."

Theodore retrieved his steaming mug of coffee, not really wanting it now. Corporate speak always did kill his appetite for anything. "Yes. But where did they go?"

Roger shrugged. "Don't know."

Theodore leaned against the counter. "Really? No indication of these grand new positions?"

"People only ever leave a job for something better."

"Think there's something better than Edison?"

Roger thunked his mug into the sink. "I wouldn't know. I've never looked." He winked at him, then headed out.

Strange. CEOs were notoriously headhunted. An O'Flannery CEO would most definitely be sought after. The fact that Roger hadn't even thought about it was … odd. Then again, Roger wasn't one for straight answers.

The guy didn't trust Theodore, and it irritated him. He'd had enough therapy to know his kryptonite was other people's uncertainty about his sincerity. Alice, too, was beginning to have doubts. It was all over her face, despite the fact she'd demanded the physical distance from him.

Edison—and his attraction to Alice—shouldn't be so complicated.

He took his unwanted coffee and headed to Samuel—one man who did trust him.

Samuel stood at the large windows, staring down at the street. "Close the door behind you, will you?" The man didn't turn around.

Theodore did what he asked and joined him at the windows.

"We suspect Roger's been skimming," Samuel said to the glass.

Surprise should have coursed through Theodore, but it didn't. "So, he's the one, eh?"

"Yes. Suzy was suspicious, and with Alice's help—"

"Alice uncovered that?"

"No."

"But you and Suzy told her, right?" They'd conscripted her to help uncover the financial mess that was Edison Tech.

"Of course not. We need to find out if he has help. Alice—"

"Spends all her day putting out fires. Haven't you noticed?"

Samuel finally faced him. "Distraction technique?"

"It's not her."

Samuel eyed him, letting a beat pass between them. Then he sucked in a long breath and returned to the table. After sitting, he inched his chin up at the chair opposite him. "Sit. Tell me what you've discovered."

Theodore then spent over an hour nailing the coffin lid on Roger's career there. His dalliances, the unhappiness of his employees—it all came out.

Samuel eyed him. "Nailing an admin here and there isn't the worst of his crimes."

"Surprising you'd say that." Maybe the man was softening his stance on office matches.

Samuel sighed heavily. "How else do we meet people, right?"

"True. So, you got an eye for someone?"

He shook his head slowly. "But you do, don't you?"

One thing about the O'Flannerys, they didn't miss a thing. "Jealous?"

Samuel chuffed. "Still into women, my friend." His eyes sliced sideways to a group of women passing by the glass wall of the conference room. Patty, Tricia, and Stephanie were parading by.

"So, about this possible embezzlement." He pounded the table with his fist. "Keep it sealed."

That meant he couldn't tell Alice.

"You've got no one to tell, right?" Samuel eyed him.

Theodore pursed his lips. "No one."

He let his chair thunk upright. "Good. Glad to see the NDA is intact."

"Wondering about my loyalty?"

"I'd never. Come on." He rose. "Drinks on me."

Shit. Samuel knew about him and Alice, and he'd been given the only warning he'd get. Talk about a rock and hard place.

He had to stay true to his NDA.

But it meant he'd have to keep Alice in the dark—a woman he very much liked and respected. She'd learn of the news eventually. He didn't have to like it, but he was legally bound to respect the terms of the NDA. He was bound by years of friendship too.

Bloody hell.

16

———

After one solo meeting with Suzy O'Flannery, Alice understood why the woman had landed on the front page of *Entrepreneur Today* magazine—four times with headlines like *Up and Coming CEO Takes Tech World By Storm* and *Shrewdest CEO on the Planet?* Now, three days into the CFO-in-training meetings, as Alice had dubbed them, she knew "shrewd" didn't even come close to covering the woman's personality.

Alice was going to have to figure out how to tell her the real story about the petty cash that was stolen. No way would Alice take the fall for Roger's made-up story when Suzy found out about it—and she would find out. However, she also didn't want Suzy to think she'd been responsible for having that much cash on hand in the first place.

Suzy tapped her lips. "See how operating cash isn't aligning with this number? Our supplier costs are down by five percent, production is up, so what do you think is happening?"

Alice stared hard again at the spreadsheet. She still couldn't understand how Edison Tech's profits were in a downward trajectory. She'd done her accounting work and made sure everything reconciled. The CFO was in charge of the higher-level reports, and when they had one, he didn't tell her half the things Suzy clued her in on. When he left? She ran them, but Roger did most of the analyzing. Then again, Roger's lie about the petty cash showed he cared little about details, only his reputation.

Alice racked her mind to come up with some response to Suzy's question. The answer plunked down into her brain. "Our cash conversion cycle is off."

"Yes. Very good." Suzy leaned back and raised her hand to hide a yawn. They'd been at it for hours. "Any plans for the upcoming weekend?"

That was another thing. The woman's mind could switch topics faster than a cheetah on the tail of a gazelle. "Oh, not much," Alice said.

"I haven't decided, either."

Alice immediately imagined the options Suzy and her brother had. Whatever it was, she suddenly had the urge to join their plans.

Maybe they'd fly in their private jet to the Hamptons and decamp to their Pinterest-worthy beach house. Then Suzy would spend the day sailing on their private sailboat in a pair of cute white cropped pants and a black-and-white striped top and have glamorous dinners at night in a flowing maxi-dress with lots of chunky gold jewelry that would clink when she raised her champagne glass to her lips.

Never mind it was still January. Alice's mind filled with the images. Strange. She *never* had those kinds of thoughts, but now she couldn't stop assessing how Suzy lived her life. One thing was for sure: She worked as hard as Alice. Harder, in fact.

Suzy closed the folder of reports. "Got a date tonight?"

Shock didn't cover what Alice felt at that moment. "N-no."

"Hmmm, you should get out more. Have fun while you can."

"I like to work."

"Well, as our new CFO, you're going to get a lot of that." She eyed Alice. "Yes." She nodded once. "I think you're going to do great things here. If we keep the company, that is."

A jolt of panic shot through Alice. "Thinking of selling?" It'd make sense, given that was what the O'Flannerys did with their ventures eventually. Plus, the recent revelations of how bad things had gotten at Edison certainly might make them dump the company. But she was so close to being an official CFO, she didn't want to leave now.

"It's not in good enough shape. But would that be a problem?"

Ah, testing her loyalty perhaps? "I love it here. I was hoping to be part of it for a long time. What can I do to get the company into good shape—both in terms of profitably and growth?"

Suzy smiled. "Good answer. I knew you were a smart one." She then rose. "I've got to run. Theodore awaits."

Alice's heart hitched. Of course, it did. All week, when she wasn't glued to every word Suzy uttered, her thoughts drifted to wondering how he was. They hadn't spoken more than a hallway hello since their near-miss against Big Whale. The copier hadn't operated consistently since. Then, again, nothing in her vicinity seemed to be operating on all cylinders except for these meetings with Suzy.

Alice straightened some papers, trying to appear casual. "I understand his interviews are over."

She tried hard to not stare across the cattle pen on the other side of the conference room door at his temp office—like she did every time she got a break. For days, women—and *some* men—paraded into his space for "interviews."

Every time his door cracked open, a longing—a *pining*—

to be near Theodore arose like a schoolgirl mooning at a David Beckham poster over her bed. It was dangerous territory. So, she'd stayed away from him. Even waited until 7 p.m. to leave so he'd be gone by the time she hustled home. He didn't stop to say goodbye, either, which didn't bother her. Uh, uh, not her. The Twins were in town, so they both needed to be professional.

Suzy rose. "I'll share today's financial revelations with the Bs over dinner." She and "the boys," as she called Samuel and Theodore, had lunch and dinners together every day and night. It appeared Theodore had a whole life outside of her. Why did that sting so much? She mentally shook it off—for the thousandth time that week.

"I really need Theodore's management take on how we got here. Soon." Suzy then, oddly, glanced at her sideways. Checking to gauge her reaction at the mention of Theodore? Or wondering if she'd had anything to do with their dismal financial performance? Neither option was good.

Alice schooled her features. "Have everything you need from me, then?"

"I do. Thanks, Alice." Suzy then left her alone in the conference room to clean up the various folders and spreadsheets and click off the widescreen projecting their accounting database.

As she was finishing organizing the room, she heard from the direction of the door, "Okay, I'm staging a jail break." Patty leaned against the door frame. "The GOAT. It's rugby appreciation something night, and you and I are going to go stare at their fine butts."

The last thing Alice wanted to do was sit on a hard bar stool at the GOAT Grill to deflect sloppy drunk thirty-something guys who played on Saturdays and thought they could have been the next Jonah Lomu "if only they had the support."

"I can't. I'm way behind on the books, and the end of month—"

"Will come and go like it does every month. But rugby night only comes during the season. Besides, something tells me what's in those," her eyes dropped to the mess of papers strewn about, "will ensure you prematurely need Botox." She pushed off her lean. "You frown any more, and I'm carting you off to Suzy O'Flannery's plastic surgeon."

"So sure she's had some?" Alice had to admit Suzy looked amazing, not that looks were everything. But honestly, if a woman wanted to freshen herself up, then she should be able to do whatever the hell she wanted with her own body.

"Not one hundred percent yet." Patty examined her manicure. "But there's no way that woman looks that good naturally, so I'm on the hunt. Ya'know, for the future. Anyway. Don't be late. I'll be in our usual spot." Patty liked the corner end of the GOAT bar, mostly so she could stare at whoever was coming in.

Alice didn't need a rugby player, but a drink did sound pretty good. Now that she was changing Edison's accounting from an accrual to a cash basis, at Suzy's request, she'd surely have more bad news to report. Why rush it?

The GOAT was packed. She never could understand the appeal of the place. It served the usual overly greasy burgers and chowders at a long bar and had strategically placed wood tables so every seat could get a look at one of the dozens of TV screens blasting various sports channels. The Greatest of All Time was etched in old English letters above the bar, and the host always welcomed patrons at the front of house with a "Welcome to the GOATs of the sports world."

"You're late." Patty slapped the bar stool next to her

dramatically. "I had to fend off two other femmes to keep this stool. And fighting is not a good look on me."

Alice put her purse on the sticky bar. "Hey, Abram, stow this for me?"

The bartender, holding two beers, lifted his chin. "Sure thing, Alice."

"How do you know his name?" Patty asked. "We haven't been out in forever."

"I remember everyone's name. Suzy says names are important." Except she hadn't remembered May Lynn's. Maybe she was slipping.

Patty groaned. "We're not going to spend all night listening to you crush on Suzy, are we? Because I need a night of pure testosterone. Ooo, like that guy." She eyed a man in a blue-and-white rugby shirt who slapped the back of another guy in a polo shirt. Naturally, her object of interest had a thick shock of black hair. The more active the hair follicles on a man, the greater Patty's desire.

Someday, Alice would have to uncover why. For now? She needed liquor. Right before she left, she'd spotted Theodore leading Tricia into the elevator with his hand on her back. Maybe Tricia scored an invitation to dinner? It'd make sense to have the head of HR there, given Theodore would be reporting his findings. Her reaction didn't. The ridiculous ache that started in her chest required tamping down.

"Shot of tequila, Abram?" she asked as he darted by.

That got Patty's attention from the "Henry Cavill" she was eyeing. "Make that two." She placed her hands on her lap. "Okay, you only drink tequila when something bad happens. Come to think of it, you've been on edge lately. It's not like you, and the office is unnerved. I mean, you're the heartbeat there."

She scoffed. "Yeah, right. Because I have jumper cables?"

More like she hadn't gotten jumped lately—by a certain management consultant. And right then, she realized what had her on pins and needles. It wasn't a bad financial report. Or even Theodore's lack of attention. It was because she'd become someone she didn't recognize. She didn't walk around like a bag of lit-up hormones. At least, not until she'd been acquainted with Kiss a Ginger Day.

"Did Suzy do something?" Patty asked. "You get as much time with the topic as it takes to throw down our first shot. Then we're talking about something else."

Talking about work *would* be better. "No. She's great. Been a kind of mentor, actually." She took the little shot glass Abram had filled for her. The golden liquid shone in the low bar light. "And she made me CFO."

Patty slapped her arm, and she nearly lost some of the tequila. "Bury the lede, will you? How cool!"

"Yeah, I guess." She shot the amber liquid back, the burn and warmth making a long trail down her throat.

"You guess? Take the win. I swear, Alice, sometimes I feel like nothing's good enough for you."

Alice dropped the glass to the bar. "What do you mean by that?"

"I mean, you're kind of a glass-isn't-the-right-kind person."

Alice dipped her chin. "What?"

"Some people are glass half full. Some half empty. You're, like, why's the glass so small? Has the glass been tested? Did we run all the data?"

Her belly twisted. "Are you saying I'm suspicious? Because that's a good thing for an accountant."

"*CFO.* And no. It's just when things are going well, you tend to doubt it. And then wonder when things will go wrong. It's why I think you're out to solve everyone's problems. You have a nose for them."

She chuffed. "If that were true, I'd have questioned our reports more over the years." She slapped a hand over her mouth. "Oops. Shouldn't have told you that."

Patty waved her hand. "I know Edison isn't doing well. I mean, the way Roger runs things …" She rolled her eyes and then squared herself to Alice. "Do you know he gave that big project with Chainlink Logistics to Daniel. Daniel! Who started six months ago. I could program circles around him."

"You're the best programmer we've got. I'm so sorry."

She sniffed. "I know." Now it was Patty's turn to chug back her tequila shot. "One more, Abram," she called. "We're about to go into how to dismantle the patriarchy."

Smirking as he did so, he had them refilled in seconds. "Best of luck to you."

Patty pursed her lips at him. "We don't need luck."

Alice lifted her glass. "To significant change at Edison."

"Yeah." She clinked her glass against Alice's. "Now, please tell me Suzy's going to quell the most out-of-control male patriarch, also known as Roger." She tsked. "Always thinking he knows better."

"I have no idea. But I can tell she's not happy with the guy. He really is the worst."

"Good." She lifted her shot glass again. "Say it with me. Here's to better days, and fuck the patriarchy."

Alice clinked her shot glass. "Fuck patriarchy privilege."

"Except Theo. He can power over me anywhere, anytime," Patty sang and swiveled on her stool.

"I hear he has an opening at 10 a.m. tomorrow. Get in line early."

"You seriously wouldn't mind if I, uh, *got in line?*"

Alice squeezed her shot glass until her fingers turned white. "Why would I mind?" she gritted out.

Patty slammed her glass down, sacrificing at least half the liquor to the bar. "I was right. You're into him."

Alice frowned, reached for a napkin. "Am not."

"Are too. You were about to throw down with me, thinking I might get under that fat fountain pen he's been using." She leaned forward. "Tell me. It's thick, isn't it?" She waggled her eyebrows.

Alice threw back her shot. She knew exactly the dimensions of his fountain pen—and what it could produce.

"Oh, I see." Patty nodded slowly. "He's been withholding his *instrument* from you." She quickly glanced down at her glass. "Abram? You're slacking here." She held out her shot glass, and he refilled them both.

Alice took the refilled glass. "Okay, but you have to keep this under your hat."

Patty straightened and adjusted her glasses. "I am the soul of discretion. Now, spill."

Patty discrete? Not true, but Alice had little choice. If she didn't get a handle on her Theodore obsession, she'd have to admit she'd finally lost her damned mind. Talk about bending to a patriarchal cliché. "I don't know what's wrong with me. I've turned into a … *lust bucket*." She whispered the last few words.

Patty gasped. She then clasped her hands together and drummed her fingers excitedly. "My girl is finally growing into her full womanhood! Oh my God, it's about time. Listen, I know all the best lubes …"

"Patty."

"Don't Patty me. I've been waiting for this day. Now we can talk about sex!" Again, with her fingers.

Alice grasped them, then lowered them to Patty's lap. "This isn't good."

Pursing her lips, Patty cocked her head. "It's what we're designed to do. Do not let a good clitoris go to waste."

"Uh, no, I think we grew out of the caves and moved into

cubicles as the good lord intended. Fuck the patriarchy, remember?"

"That means we don't grovel at the ego altar. This, however"—she pointed at her crotch—"must be serviced to be healthy. I don't know why you're upset. He seems to be a really good guy. And he's into you. I can tell. Have a fling. Enjoy life."

"I don't want to be just a fling." She could admit it. When she thought about getting out into the world more, having more balance, she didn't want to have casual flings. She wanted National BAE Day—every day. Theodore introduced her to the concept, and now she couldn't stop thinking about what it'd be like. But Theodore was on the road all the time, and he clearly loved women. The logical conclusion was he was merely interested in having fun.

For one, as much as Theodore talked about waiting in the beginning, how they'd delay acting on their chemistry until his management consulting gig was up so they didn't have to sneak around, she'd allowed their attraction to one another get out of control. She didn't indulge in out-of-control anything—ever. Until she did. Dammit. He was not good for her. Not at all.

"The truth is," Alice said. "My New Year's resolution is to take control of my destiny, not let things happen *to* me. The thing with Theodore is too ... out of my control."

"It's just new to you," Patty sighed. "Besides, you can't control love."

"We've known each other for two weeks."

"Insta-love. My favorite!"

Patty fell in love regularly, so her assessment wasn't reassuring. "That makes no sense. It has to be just an office dalliance in his mind. I tried. For one weekend—"

"I knew it. Stroll around the Jefferson my very fine ass.

You were coming up for air. But go on, go on." She crooked her fingers, clearly wanting more.

"I can't. Go on, that is."

"Have you asked him? Point blank? Is this only an office fling? Are you dating anyone else? Am I the only one? Can I be the only one? Because, trust me, if he runs for the hills from you asking those questions, you got your answer. If he answers the way you want, which I take it would be no-no-yes-yes, then you get what you want." She shrugged like it was the simplest thing in the world.

Alice's head swam. She could barely match up Patty's "no-no-yes-yes" to the questions.

She'd almost outright asked him, with Big Whale as a witness, but then it seemed silly to ask him to nail down something she didn't even fully understand.

"Do it," Patty urged. "Call him right now, Miss Control My Destiny."

"What? No."

"True, not from a bar. Go to the ladies' room. It's quieter."

"No. He might think …"

"What? That *you're* into him? Maybe he's been waiting for a sign from you."

What Patty didn't know was Alice had pretty much thrown herself at him a few times. He took her up on her offer, but then what red-blooded guy wouldn't? Maybe he thought *she* was using *him*.

Alice scratched her head. "I'm so confused."

Patty hopped off the stool, grabbed Alice's hands, and forced her to stand. "Then go get unconfused. I'll hold the bar stool. That brunette over there keeps eyeing us, waiting for us to fall off them so she can nab them. Not on my watch. So, hurry." Patty pushed her toward the ladies' room.

Alice made her way slowly. Her head swam a bit, thanks

to the tequila. It'd been at least seven hours since she'd had food, and tequila always made her loopy.

Of course, there was a line to the bathroom. Maybe she could text him. She unlocked her phone.

<<**Hi. Watch doing?**>> Stupid auto correct, changing "watcha" to "watch."

Floating dots appeared. <<**7:20. Think it's a bit slow.**>>

He was teasing her. But at least he'd answered. <<**Busy?**>>

<<**Me or my watch?**>>

Heat built in her belly. She was tired of him turning everything into a joke—or a national whatever day. <<**Hard hard**>> Shit. She meant to write har-har. "Damn you, auto correct."

"Happens to me all the time," a woman next to her who was leaning against the concrete wall said to her. "Boyfriend?"

"No. A maybe."

"Yeah, I got some of those, too."

Alice didn't really want to know about anyone else's love life. She had her hands full with her own. Thankfully, it was the woman's turn to go into the ladies' room next, so she left Alice standing alone in the hallway.

Alice lifted her phone when it pinged. Theodore had answered.

<<**Not hard yet but keep texting me and it won't take long.**>>

The man also turned everything into sex. Then again, so had she.

She furiously typed back in case she lost her nerve. <<**What are we drawing?**>> *Fuck. Fuck. Fuck.* <<**DOING**>> She might as well launch into it, as Patty had suggested.

<<**Sexting. Which might be awkward, given Samuel is sitting next to me.**>>

Dammit. <<**No, we're not. Not now.**>> There. She took control.

<<**If only that message worked with my growing hard-on.**>>

<<**Samuel turn you on?**>>

<**Knowing you're on the other end of the phone does.**>>

He really could be charming. <<**Are you dating anyone else?**>> She had to keep her head, now swimming a little, focused on the task at hand. A row of infuriatingly blinky dots floated on her screen. Then they just disappeared.

Ghosting her? Ha. She angrily typed out his number and raised it to her ear. A rustle of fabric sounded. "Well, this is awkward," he said.

She knew it. He had someone else. She was an office fling. No, worse. She was the office *sweet butt*—the girl passed around among the motorcycle gang members. Tequila always had ignited the strangest part of her imagination, but there was no stopping the spiral. Her thoughts ran over one another like lemmings seeking their death off the cliff.

"Awkward? Why? Because you *are* dating someone else?" she gritted out as she caught the swinging ladies' room door as the woman left. Good, because she really, really needed to pee.

"Tell me the truth. You have a woman in every office, don't you?" She regretted her tone the instant the words came out. She should hang up. Take the time to gather her more logical thoughts.

"Yes. There are women in every office I've ever been in." More laughter came from him.

She balanced the phone on the toilet roll holder and angrily hiked up her skirt. She didn't know why she was suddenly so irritated. How about because he thought it was one big joke?

"Alice, Alice." Theodore's voice sounded very far away.

"Wait a minute, I'm peeing." She let it fly. If he couldn't handle a little reality, then tough noogies, as her dad used to say.

No more words from Theodore came through the phone.

She leaned forward and got her ear close to the phone. "Oh, so you're silent now?"

"Seemed proper, considering Niagara Falls has got nothing on you." His low chuckle ratcheted up her anger.

"Oh, funny guy. Well, get used to it because real women pee." She reached for some toilet paper, and her phone promptly fell to the ground. "Dammit." She finished, yanked her panties back up, and grabbed her phone. "Ewww, disgusting." Dark streaks lined the glass—grime from the bathroom floor.

She held it a safe distance from her ear as she exited the stall. Two women stood there, staring at her aghast. She pointed at her phone. "Dropped it. Mid fight with the guy I've unwisely slept with at work."

It was time to start telling the truth everywhere.

"Happens all the time," one of the women said.

And that was the problem. It might happen to other people, just not to her.

"Alice, Alice!" Theodore called.

She quickly cleaned her phone, which essentially killed the call. He rang back in seconds and didn't wait for her to say anything when she accepted it. "Where are you?"

"The GOAT. With Patty. Meeting all kinds of hot rugby guys." The floor was floating a little. She tried to stop swaying with it.

"I'm coming to get you." Theodore killed the call.

She stared at her phone. "Oh, really? We'll see about that."

She took her time washing her hands. She needed a minute to assess the situation. Her brain was having none of it, refusing to have one single coherent thought. Time to call it a night.

When she got back to the bar, Patty had been true to her word, with her legs propped up on Alice's seat.

"Well." Patty dramatically swung her legs back toward the bar. "I see you got your answer."

"Don't let my face fool you." She dropped to the seat and swiveled her head to the bartender. "I need water, Abram."

Patty held up her phone. "Theodore says he'll recommend I get put on the Chainlink project immediately if I keep you here until he arrives."

"What?"

She shrugged. "He called. I negotiated. Now, get comfortable because I will tie you to this bar if you make one move for the door. I'm going to program circles around Daniel."

Alice closed her eyes, which was an epic mistake. She nearly toppled from her seat. She snapped them open to find Patty smiling over at her.

"Told ya' about Theodore," she said. "*Insta-love.*"

17

____

Theodore clung to edge of the bed. His nips were frozen from the night air, but his back was on fire. Alice was glued against him as tight as a starfish, her arm banded around his chest. It was nice—soft female flesh pressed against his.

He couldn't say how she got naked in the middle of the night. Then again, the woman jerked, tossed, yanked covers, and generally thrashed about all night, taking up most of the bed space. Her clothes may have fled in survival mode.

Another crackling snore sounded behind him, followed by her throat giving off half a choking sound. He cocked his head and waited to see if she'd settle again. Apparently, the woman had a lot of tequila last night. "I hope you hold hair because this one is going to kiss the porcelain goddess soon," Patty had declared when he'd arrived at that utterly fake rugby bar.

But Alice hadn't shown any signs of throwing up. Probably because she was oddly pissed off at him. He would never understand a women's ability to flip an emotional switch at the speed of light.

First, she'd glared at him as he strode inside the dive, and then she'd promptly fainted when he'd gotten near her. The fainting thing she did was beginning to concern him.

He got her to his rental car where she came to—sort of. She refused to talk. Instead, she stared out his window, which was cracked so she could have air and he could freeze his balls off. At her front door, she'd said, "You're dismissed," with a wave of her hand as she floundered with her keys with the other. He finally grasped her hand and got the door open. She then fumbled her way to bed and passed out on top— fully clothed.

He spent a few minutes debating whether he should leave or not. In the end, given the way she drooled onto her comforter, staying was prudent.

Plus, seeing her surrounded last night by all those wannabe rugby players assessing her called up a possessive feeling. He recognized the questions simmering in their eyes. Could they get her alone? Would she go home with them? One, in particular, had been inching closer just as he'd arrived, and Theodore had nearly crawled out of his skin.

Now, he was flush against her nude body and wanting nothing more than to bury himself in her. All week he'd been tortured. She'd barely given him a passing glance. If she'd wanted to grow his interest in her with reverse psychology, her tactic worked beautifully.

Another window-rattling snore rumbled against his back as she leaned more heavily against him. His hand reached down to touch the floor—more to keep himself in the bed. But then she shifted again. He struggled to gain more purchase on the mattress, pitching his hips backward to get her to move back already.

A protest left her throat, and then a gasp. He attempted to twist to face her when she shoved him—hard. His ass hung off the bed, and all balance was lost. Arms grasping at the sheets, he once more thunked to the floor.

"Ffyc me," he cried as his bare skin hit the rough carpet. The floor covering had to be made of the same material they used to make boot brush mats.

Alice's mascara-stained, red-rimmed eyes stared down at him. "Wha—? Who's there?" She ran a hand through her matted hair.

"It is I, the fool. Kicked out of bed again." He sighed and got to his feet. His trunks hung low, with one leg scrunched up his thigh. Something else was hanging low, too. He adjusted himself.

"Why are you in your underwear?" she asked through gritted teeth before gasping again. "Why am I naked?"

"Hell if I know. You had clothes on when I put you in bed. And I'm not naked." He snapped the waistband of his trunks. "Wasn't going to ruin my suit."

"How *dare you*. Why are you here at all?"

"Excuse me, Miss Snored All Night, for wanting to make sure you were okay while waiting for you to kiss the goddess or whatever." He leaned over to the chair where he'd abandoned his clothes last night and grabbed his shirt. Now that she was awake, it was time to get coffee going. He already knew tea was a lost cause in that flat.

"Kiss? What?" She looked around the room. "Oh. Kiss the porcelain …" She suddenly stilled. And almost immediately began kicking at the sheets to free her legs. She ran around the bed and made it as far as where he stood. Then she leaned over and upchucked all over his shorts and his shirt.

He tried to jut backward, but it was too late. He bit back a string of curses and reached for her. Her eyes grew wide as saucers, then she bolted for the bathroom.

At the sight of his shorts, his stomach lurched in protest, but he managed to tamp it down. After abandoning them and his now-ruined shirt in her overflowing laundry basket— dear God, let her have a washing machine—he headed to

Alice. Duty called. By the sounds coming out of her bathroom, she was making love to the toilet.

He grabbed a too-small towel from the rack just inside the bathroom door and wrapped it around himself. It barely clung to his torso as he knelt beside her. He grasped her hair and began to rub circles on her back as she emptied her stomach. After a few minutes, it stopped.

She pulled back and leaned against the tub. "I always wanted a man who held my hair. It's not what it's cracked up to be. It's humiliating."

"I've seen worse. Granted, usually outside a pub in Westminster, but …"

"Stop trying to make me feel better. I'm mad at myself. And you."

"For being a natural redhead?" The towel didn't stand a chance. His goods were now out in all their glory.

She frowned. "For turning me into a nymphet."

"I've done no such thing. Though"—he waved his hand over his crotch—"I am hard to resist." He sat down next to her, his towel coming loose. What the hell. Let it all hang out. It wasn't like they hadn't seen all of each other.

She slammed the toilet seat closed and flushed it. "Stop playing dumb, Theodore."

A bubble of anger rose in his chest. "What is going on with you?" No way in hell was he leaving until he learned why she was so angry with him.

"You will not turn me into the office *sweet butt*."

What the devil was she talking about? "The what?"

Again, her hand waved in the air. "I can't do this back and forth with you anymore. It's not who I am. I'm finally getting a little ahead at work. I can't have my mind"—she glanced down at his penis which was starting to wake up—"elsewhere. So, towel, please?"

He re-adjusted the towel so it semi-covered him. "Is that

what all your messages were about last night? You think I've turned you in to the office … slut butt?" Rather rescued her from a horrific bar last night.

"*Sweet* butt, and yes. Sort of." She rubbed her eyes and groaned. "I can't do it. Suzy told me I should be Edison's CFO. That's all I should be thinking about. Not wondering who you're with. Watching you flirt all week with everyone." She batted her eyelashes. "*Oh, Linda, you look so nice today. Oh, Tricia, let me help you into the elevator.*"

A laugh burst from his throat. He'd never understand the opposite sex. They want someone friendly, but when you actually be that? Suddenly, you were about to nail everything with ovaries within five miles.

She smacked his arm in response. "I see how you are with all these women. Yet you say you want to have National BAE Day with me? You have a funny way of showing it."

He rubbed his bicep. The woman had some muscle on her. "Hey, you were the one who wanted us to be professional." Hurt crossed her eyes. Again, women and their ricocheting thoughts and feelings. "Look, now is not the time to talk about this. You need coffee and breakfast." He rose, the towel slipping completely to the floor. He grabbed it.

She peered up at his cock. "Changing the subject?"

"Yes, because I don't even know what subject we're really on. I'm on four hours of sleep, so forgive me if I'm a little slow on the uptake." He softened his voice. "Tell me what you want to know."

She sucked in a short breath. "Am I just an office affair?"

Of course, that was what she was getting at. "To have an office affair, we would actually have to be fucking."

"We have been."

"Oh, really? Not nearly enough." He pointed to his semi hard-on. "This has been neglected, I'll have you know. One more thought about what it's like to be inside you, and my penis is going to explode. You have no idea the effect you have on me."

She pointed down at her own crotch and pursed her lips. "Mine, too, you know." Then she crossed her arms in defiance.

He scrubbed his hair. His brain was beginning to throb in pain. "You know, most people in the world look for this kind of attraction. They don't resist it."

"Most people weren't just promoted to CFO by Suzy O'Flannery. Expectations on how I behave have risen."

"Congratulations, by the way."

"Thank you."

"But you can have a life, too. And I say we need to stop this."

Her gaze sliced his way, her lips parting. More hurt grew in her eyes. Jesus, what did he keep saying?

"I agree," she whispered.

"Good, then no more resisting it. We should be going at it like rabbits. I can't keep thinking about you across those cubicles in your tight little skirts. Which I'm convinced you wear to drive me crazy. I can barely concentrate." It had been hard. Every time he heard her voice or saw her sashay by his office, his whole body seemed desperate to get to her.

Even now with her face blotchy, her eyes red-rimmed and glassy, he'd bury himself in her in two minutes if she allowed it. Alice was hot, but more than that, she was quick and had a mind of her own—a rare intelligence that kept his mind as active as his penis. The combination was lethal.

"Me, too. And I'm not happy about it," she gritted out as if it were the biggest burden in the world to want him.

There was only one thing to do. "Then, it's settled. Every time we feel like it, we need to do it." Their attraction to one another couldn't be contained. Why fight it at all? In fact, what on earth made either of them think they could wait until June?

She crossed her arms, which only brought his attention to her breasts. "Oh, really?'

"Yes. As you pointed out, it's unnatural to be carrying around this much lust." Some days, he felt like his insides were on fire. He was surprised the sprinklers in the ceiling hadn't turned on.

"But only with each other, right?"

He'd been right. She was worried about fidelity. He held out his hand. "Deal. Exclusive lust sating."

When she tentatively grasped his handshake, he pulled her to standing. Her nude body immediately pressed against him and they stared at one another for a long minute, which only gave his semi hard-on time to go fully erect.

"You said something about coffee," she finally said.

"I did." Neither moved. His head began to dip to her mouth when she broke free, yanking on the water and grabbing her toothbrush.

She vigorously brushed her teeth and stared at him in the mirror.

He drew closer, his hard-on pressing against the small of her back. He may be sleep-deprived and confused as hell as to what just happened, but he'd go with it.

When she was done, she twisted to face him. He brushed hair from her face. "Hey, I declare it Take Care of Alice Day. And we're done putting any parameters on things. We go with it."

"But we keep it to ourselves. No telling anyone at the office."

She wanted it, but wanted it alone with him? Perfect by him. "They're not invited to what I want to do to you."

Finally, he got a smile out of her—and she nodded in agreement. No more resistance.

They would be late as hell to work.

18

Alice's hands roamed his back, her fingertips brushing along the curve of his spine. Studying him. Every time they came together, she noticed something new. Like how the freckles scattered across his shoulders deepened in color as his skin grew more flushed. How they formed a pattern like a constellation.

Theodore stilled. "Breathe."

She sucked in air, her chest barely moving under the weight of him.

He growled, nipped along her jawline, and began to move again. He'd been doing that for over an hour—bringing her up to the precipice only to pause, telling her to breathe, telling her how beautiful she looked pricked with perspiration and panting. Her "glowing" had to be exertion from holding back a tsunami of an orgasm.

"Theodore, please." She never took herself for someone who begged. But at that point, she didn't care he pulled pleas out of her so easily. An overbearing urge to get him as deep as possible overrode any pride.

His hands twisted in her hair and pulled her head back to expose her neck. "Let's take the day off."

"Can't." The word was barely a puff of air.

"Drill sergeant. Or is that me?" His hips once more pitched into her, and he licked his lips as if he were about to take a bite of her.

She giggled. "That would be you drilling." Why not give into the juvenile humor? They acted like horny teenagers anyway.

He pulled out, grasped under her knees, and yanked her farther down the bed until her calves hung down the side. His gaze roamed her body once more. The raw heat blazing in his blue eyes was like he was taking her in for the first time again. It was so fucking hot. The man wanted her. Like *really* wanted her.

He dropped to his knees and roughly parted her legs. She was so exposed; a sliver of embarrassment threatened to rise. But then he dove in and sucked hard on her clit.

"Oh, my God," she cried out. There was no easing in of things with Theodore. The man gave her no time to react. Two of his thick fingers began thrusting in and out of her as he licked relentlessly.

Her back arched in a huge convulsion of sensation. She was sure he'd have to peel her off the ceiling.

He didn't wait for her to come down. He crawled up her body and entered her as the last waves of her orgasm fluttered inside her. "So. Ffycing. Good," he growled into her neck.

She stared up at him, amazed. And maybe a little in love. Or it was just the oxytocin flooding her system. Either way, she couldn't deny the warm glow in her chest. But she needed to keep it in perspective. Real love complicated things.

Still, her mind spun. Would it always be like that between

them? Their bodies vibrating against one another? So in sync?

His mouth was on hers again, kissing her deeply as he pulsed inside her, giving in himself. When he released his kiss, his hot breath brushed over her face and his blue eyes drank her in.

"Beautiful." He brushed damp hair from her face. His words increased the happiness blooming behind her ribs.

She bit her tongue in case she said something unwise—like the L word. She couldn't be in love with him. It was merely the oxytocin coursing through her body.

Cold air washed over her chest as he dropped beside her. He was panting as much as she was. They both stared at the ceiling for a long minute, neither caring they were over an hour late to Edison Tech.

He threw his arm over his eyes. "You're going to have to shower alone," he said to the room. "We'll never get out of this apartment if I keep looking at you naked."

"Good idea." She might be tempted to lie in bed all day, otherwise. "You first, though." She was desperate for water and then coffee.

She rose, clutching the damp sheet to her breasts. Her modesty was stupid. He'd seen everything at that point. *Tasted* everything.

While he showered alone, she picked out the day's outfit, a plain black skirt and a crisp white shirt. Nothing that might give Theodore ideas once they got to the office. She had a boatload of work to do.

She made a bowl of yogurt and granola and a pot of coffee. She also texted Patty and Tricia and told them she'd be in a little late. "More than a little late," she muttered. Neither texted back right away, so she headed to her bathroom to extricate Theodore. The man was a shower hog.

Just as she got near, he cracked open her bathroom door. A cloud of steam surrounded him as he stepped out.

"Were you reading *War and Peace* in there?" she teased.

"Taking care of business. All I could think about was you being out here naked and alone."

"Tell me you didn't." How could he beat one out after their sexual gymnastics?

"It took a bit, but I managed."

The man was a sexual neanderthal. How many orgasms could a man have in one day? "You have any skin left down …." She dipped her chin down toward his crotch.

"Nope. Thanks to you."

Gah. *The nerve.* "I'll have you know, I'm lucky I have a vagina left." She was sore. Damn, she should have gotten cranberry juice the last time she was at the store. Which was when, exactly? Her routines were so off since Theodore Gaston *the Fourth* had arrived.

"Anything I can do to help lubricate the tissues?"

"Don't you dare." They really had to get to Edison. "I'll only be twenty minutes." Fifteen, if she didn't shave her whole leg.

True to her word, they finally were out the door twenty minutes later. Her hair, still wet, was twisted up in a messy bun, and she wore her black skirt and white shirt.

"Well, great," Theodore muttered as he locked the door behind her. "Now I'm going to have sexy librarian fantasies all day." He turned and let his gaze scan her from head to toe.

He moved to advance on her, but she slapped her palm on his chest. "We are so late."

He grasped her hand, lifted it to his mouth, and kissed the back of it. "You sure you don't want to take the day off?"

For half a second, she was tempted. But then, as if her conscience were trying to reach her, her phone pinged in her purse. "See? Someone needs something."

"Got that all from the chime, did you?"

"Those are the only calls or texts I get."

His brows furrowed a little. "I call."

"Ah, but you're work. Technically, anyway."

He slapped his chest, dropping his chin. "Relegated to the work zone. I'm crushed." He raised his lids, his baby blues twinkling toward her.

"Okay, you're more than that."

"More than." He yanked her forward, so her captured hand was the only thing separating their bodies. "You are most definitely more than."

His eyes bore down on her. She had to remind herself not to read anything into the little sparkles that danced there. But seeing how intently he gazed at her, the traitorous glow in her chest grew to the size of the sun. It nearly knocked her off her feet.

She swallowed. "I'll see you at the office, though?"

"I'll make a point of it." His wicked grin ruined yet another pair of her panties. Her reaction to him was uncanny.

And that golden light inside her chest? It didn't get any smaller—not when she got in her car. Not when she drove the fifteen minutes to Edison and found her favorite parking spot occupied with Roger's car of all things. And not when she stepped off the elevator and into the usual cattle pen chaos.

In fact, she barely heard anyone as she made her way to her office, plunked herself down, and turned on her computer.

More than kept swimming in her mind. She'd never been *more than* to anyone before.

She glanced up every time the elevator door dinged across the large office space. Theodore stepped out on the fifth time the doors opened. His eyes searched the space quickly and found hers. Even from across the cattle pen, she could see the warmth in his smile. He was happy to see her.

But then he abruptly broke the eye lock and headed toward the conference room.

That was good. Yes, she reminded herself. It was good they were both at work and hadn't tumbled back into bed. That they'd gone to their separate corners of the office.

Of course, the self-imposed celibacy only lasted until three in the afternoon. That was when he unwisely chose to slip into her office and ask how she was doing. Five minutes later, door locked and blinds drawn on the large glass window, he laid her across her desk. Her skirt was pushed up around her hips and her white blouse was opened so he could suck on her breasts through the lace fabric of her bra.

Like rabbits, he'd once told her. It was true. The little critters of the world would have been proud of them.

19

———

Alice had never regretted focusing on her career. But now that she had a life? She should have made more room for one. If "having a life" meant having sex during the day—at Edison. It was thrilling and, while dangerous, somehow sharpened her senses. It wasn't a bad thing, given she was now working with Suzy.

She and Theodore had started by going out to lunch in an effort to take their desire for one another out of the office. But they could never make it to the restaurant. Once, they'd parked in a secluded spot in a parking garage across town. She'd climbed onto his lap and rode him senseless. Another time, they made it to a park after finding a parking spot behind some large bushes. Both times, they were late as hell back to the office.

Now they didn't dare leave together during the day for fear of taking too long. Instead, the supply room would have to do when the mood struck. And strike it did—often. Hardly anyone ever went in there besides her, anyway.

The tiny space had a lock on the door, which was handy and necessary. The fact that it also had a nice corner niche where he could hold her up against the wall was a bonus. He often had to put his hand over her mouth to stifle her cries, which only turned her on more.

The copier room also proved useful once. She'd never been so glad to have Edison's government contracts require secure copying space as she had in that moment. She'd slipped the "Do Not Enter" sign on the door, locked it, then sat on the Formica table while he stood pitching into her so hard black marks marred the wall behind it. Thank God, it was an outside wall because *noise*. And Big Whale didn't protest once.

But it was risky, and she put the kibosh on that location.

Then, today? They were passing one another in the hallway, outside the supply room. His blue eyes did their sparkling magic, and she found herself slipping inside the tiny space, hoping Theodore would follow. He did.

Alice kicked off her panties as soon as the click on the door sounded. "We have to be quick."

Theodore stalked to her and circled his hand around the back of her neck, a move she'd grown increasingly fond of. "Got a plane to catch or something?" He went to work on his trousers with his free hand. The clank of his belt buckle sounded in the air.

"A Suzy meeting. So, yeah, a meeting with a 747." She flipped up her flouncy skirt. She'd abandoned anything too tight days ago.

Lowering his zipper, he drew himself out. "I got your 747 right here." After slipping on a condom, which he now carried with him, he wasted no time moving into her slowly. He took pleasure in driving her crazy that way, taking his sweet time filling her up. A long sigh rumbled up her throat.

"I do love the way you sigh when I enter you the first time," he whispered into her hair.

She licked her lips. "I like all times."

"Like this one?" He pushed in again, slowly.

"Yes," she breathed.

His hand circled her thigh, lifted her leg. "Or this?" He thrust into her harder.

"I think I need to gather more data. Have more …" Her words failed her.

His hand released her neck, moving to her other leg and yanking it higher so he could hold her by her thighs. God, he was strong. She had to put both hands on the back wall to steady herself.

He buried himself to the hilt, and she groaned at the delicious spread inside.

Words found her again. "Fuck me."

"With pleasure." His mouth came down on hers, knowing when he ground into her faster and faster, her cries would start. Her animal response to him was easily explained. The man was spectacular at sex. Like he had a map of her body memorized, knew every spot that drove her wild, and explored it with abandon. He had a photographic memory, after all.

His own rumblings started, and a possessive thrill ran up her spine at the sound. Pride she was the one he was fucking into oblivion in the supply closet spread like wildlife. She saw the way other women looked at him. But she was the one …

Over the last few days, a happy, gooey feeling had settled in her chest. The glow, as she'd labeled it, was like immersing herself in a warm bath. It was relaxing. No thinking. Just feeling. Sating a relentless biological need. She and Theodore had declared they shouldn't be resisting each other any longer, so who was she to stop nature from taking its course?

The room quickly grew hot and her skin clammy. She cried her climax into his shoulder, and he shook against her.

They took a second to catch their breath, and then he let her slip to the floor. She landed on her feet.

He panted into her hair. "I'm going to need at least a few hours to recover from that one."

"Recover, as in …" She arched an eyebrow.

"I rather thought we could try all our secret places in one day." He brushed hair off her face.

"Ambitious."

"More like …" He didn't finish his sentence, just stared into her eyes.

"More? You want more?" she teased, grabbing his ass and pulling him toward her. His cock was slick with her and probably ruining her skirt.

"Always more." He kissed her.

Someone rattled the supply closet door. Then a hushed whisper. "Alice. Alice." It was Patty.

Crap. So much for their secrecy. Of course, she'd spilled the beans to Patty one afternoon when Patty had caught them coming out of the copier room together. She said it was a one-off—and it had been … at least in that place. Alice gave as few details as possible, but she might have slipped that his skills fell in the category of "can't say no."

Theodore disposed of the condom in a trash bag, tucked himself away and pushed his shirt tails back into his trousers. "And that's our cue."

"Patty won't say anything to anyone."

He yanked his belt back together. "Not worried." He placed a hand by her head, caging her anew. "I'd be more worried if someone took our spot here. Harrison's got a thing for her." He winked at her.

"I know. But Harrison's got no hair."

"Shallow."

The sting at her friend mixed with the sentiment he was

right. Still, his assessment of Patty irked her, but she let it go. "A girl's gotta follow her chemistry, right?"

He unlocked the door. "It's only natural."

Patty stood on the other side with her arms crossed. "It would be so much easier if you two kept a schedule. I needed new batteries for my mouse twenty minutes ago."

Theodore merely grinned down at her. "How's Chainlink Logistics going?"

Her face softened. "Great now that I'm on it, too." She pushed past him and went into the supply closet. "God, please put air freshener on your list, Alice." She pivoted to smile back at her.

Alice stuck her tongue out at her.

Patty waved at her. "Ewww. I don't know where that's been, so keep it yourself."

Theodore chuckled as he sauntered away, shaking his head.

Well, see you later to you, too. She glanced up at the big wall clock. Shit, she was a minute late to Suzy. She only hoped Suzy wasn't as perceptive as Patty in the sex department.

Suzy sat at the conference room table, which she commandeered most days. Something about needing space. Alice thought it was so she could spy on everyone wandering the hallways. Or perhaps eyeing Roger's office door, usually closed, across the cubicle farm. Alice got the sense Suzy wasn't a Roger fan, which was odd, given she and her brother had placed him as CEO.

She strode in. "Hi, sorry I'm late."

Suzy waved her hand without looking up. "How many times a week do you do a full back-up of the accounting files?" She took off her reading glasses and chewed on the end.

"Weekly. Every Friday. Why?" She took the seat across from her.

Suzy leaned back in the chair. "Hmmm. Samuel was right."

"Of course, I was." Samuel strode in carrying a cup of coffee. He lifted it at seeing Alice. "Thanks for the new shipment of Kona, by the way."

"Sure."

"So, did you fill her in?" he asked Suzy.

"I was just about to. Close the door, will you?"

Samuel obliged, then took a seat next to his sister.

Suzy studied Alice for one long awkward moment, then rested her elbows on the table, steepling her fingers under chin. "Roger has been embezzling."

Alice froze. She blinked as if that might clear the buzzing rising in her ears. "He what?"

Samuel scratched at his hairline. "That was quite a lead-in, sis."

"Not pussy footing around anymore. We need to act swiftly."

"Could have done that two weeks ago when I found it," he chuckled into his cup.

Alice had no idea what they were talking about. Embezzlement? "I'm not sure I understand. Are some books missing? Maybe I didn't forward everything."

"Oh, you sent everything," Suzy said. "But there are discrepancies."

A slither of fear snaked up her spine. She was super careful to make sure everything reconciled every day. How could there be anything amiss?

She swallowed thickly. "Discrepancies?"

Samuel thunked upright in his chair. "Roger has been

copying the files, doctoring them, and re-uploading them. You didn't notice anything?"

"Well, sometimes, and I brought it to him. But then things went back into the black. Of course, I'd review it every weekday, so he'd have to do it on the weekend and then, I have to confess something…" She stopped her rambling. Suzy's eyes had narrowed, and she and Samuel exchanged glances.

Alice cleared her throat. It was now or never. "The petty cash that was stolen? It was thousands, not hundreds as Roger said. I should have told you earlier but—"

Suzy raised her hand and Alice snapped her lips closed. "I know. I've been waiting for you to tell me."

Samuel rested his elbows on the table, and clasped his hands together. "Alice, you didn't notice anything, like unexplained, large expenditures?"

"There are always large expenses."

Samuel nodded his head. "Sure were. Rolexes, cars, restaurants."

Alice's lips parted on a gasp.

Suzy waved her hand. "Plus, his house is mortgaged to the hilt. Georgetown real estate isn't cheap."

Alice swallowed thickly. "I should have caught it. I apologize. I wasn't aware of this situation." She might as well show some responsibility in an act of self-preservation. She wouldn't have them believe she was in on Roger's theft.

"You weren't operating with the right books. Minor changes had been made. But the matter of the false vendors was not minor. It'd take a deep investigation to catch it." Suzy then gave her an unexpected, understanding smile, and heat rose on Alice's face. It humiliated her that she wasn't capable of catching that files were being doctored. It was her job, for God's sake, to make sure numbers were right.

Alice tried hard to cool the rising shame growing up her spine. "How did you catch it?"

"I didn't." Suzy turned to her brother. "Few people know Samuel was once a forensic accountant."

Theodore strode in. "I knew Samuel was. Most boring job in the world."

"I'd say catching thieves is worth the tedium." Samuel yawned.

Theodore mock-gasped and slapped his chest. "I only swiped one bottle of your sake from your stash the other night. That's a misdemeanor, at best."

What the hell were they talking about? Other night? When? She shook her head a little to focus. "But … how could I not have noticed? How long has this been going on?" She couldn't let go of the fact that Roger's stealing was under her nose.

"We've been watching the books for about a year," Samuel said.

A fucking year?

Samuel pointed at Suzy's laptop—as if she could see through the screen and understand better? "As far as we can tell, he did a little doctoring over the weekend. Copy the file, upload a new one. Everything reconciles, but expenses show a little higher each week. Yet nothing justified it—except for some artfully crafted withdrawals."

Of course. Alice forwarded financial reports every Friday to The Twins via email, per Roger's instructions. Never Monday, he'd said. Only Friday. Now, it was making sense. On Monday, things would have looked different.

Occasionally, an email would land in her inbox from the O'Flannerys asking to see the files. She'd send them along, too, but sometimes didn't get to it until Monday or Tuesday. It never occurred to her to tell Roger about the requests. So, she could see how they'd see the discrepancies from Friday to the next week if they were looking.

For her, however? Mondays were slammed with all kinds

of things. Alice didn't spend a great deal of time scratching her head over minor changes she *thought* she'd seen but had dismissed. She'd chalked it up to being so tired by Friday she must have remembered the numbers differently.

Samuel scratched his chin, the sound too loud in her ear. "Then there's the matter of returning purchases for the cash. Still can't believe people have cash on them."

"Right?" Theodore asked him. "National Cash Back Day isn't even until November."

"Date?"

"The second."

Alice glanced up at Theodore. His presence hadn't really registered with her. Then again, she was surprised she could think at all, given how Alice's brain spun.

"I'm sorry we didn't let you in on the investigation," Suzy added. "But you were instrumental in discovering what was really going along. You being named CFO scared him." Glee colored her voice. "It made him start, let's say, taking more drastic measures. Like stealing the petty cash. Then, when you were *actually* promoted? Well …"

An awkward beat passed. There was so much to unravel in Suzy's words. Roger had been the thief of the petty cash box and his own goddamned pen. But worse? She was only made CFO to apply some heat. Roger knew how fastidious she was. She wasn't promoted on her own merit, after all.

"I see," she said slowly.

"But I knew I could count on you." Suzy placed a hand on her shoulder, and Alice had to work hard to not pull back out of hurt. "We didn't let you in on it because we couldn't afford an entrapment scenario."

Entrapment?

"Setting him up for the fall," Suzy answered her unasked question. "We just let nature take its course." Her eyes glowed. She was truly enjoying the moment.

Alice turned to Theodore. "Is that why you're here?"

"Theodore's not at liberty to say," Samuel filled in for him.

Theodore didn't say anything, and it appeared as if he wouldn't. Rather, his face was as placid as a mountain lake.

"However, that's not why this place is falling apart, is it?" Suzy asked him.

Suzy's question made her head swivel back to her. "Falling apart?" Alice had done a valiant job of holding it all together. She wasn't a martyr by any stretch of the imagination, but she'd like a little credit for doing what needed to be done.

"We know about the lack of support here for employees. And about Roger's dalliances," she said carefully.

Samuel and Theodore must have sensed her discomfort as Theodore took her arm. "But that's for another day," he said. "Today, we have a changing of the guard."

God, here comes the demotion. It would be more humiliating than being passed over in the first place. Nothing screamed incompetent like being sent down the corporate ladder.

Suzy clapped her hands. "You got that right. Let's talk new CEO. That's what matters now."

That was it? What about CFO? Alice didn't ask.

You know what? At that second, she didn't care. Being told you were advanced for a sting operation, well, stung. She could get a job elsewhere after having worked for the Golden Twins. Perhaps they'd give her a good reference.

"Roger isn't a good chief officer, embezzlement or not," Suzy continued. "We're replacing him. In fact, I might step in."

Samuel chuffed and rose. "Like you have the time. I'm off to find coffee."

"I like it around here. We have a stellar CFO, after all." Suzy beamed at her.

She should feel relieved by Suzy's faith—if it were real.

Instead, a sadness crept in. Her limbs grew too heavy on her body. It was a strange reaction. Alice should love Suzy as head of Edison. She was fun but smart. Direct but not mean. And she listened to Alice. But the fact that Alice wasn't allowed to know about their secret setup niggled at her enthusiasm.

Suzy rose. "Alice, will you give us a minute?"

She nodded, her tongue too numb to speak. She closed the door behind her just in time to hear Suzy's next words.

"Now, Theodore, about you and Alice …."

20

Suzy cocked her head, pursed her lips. "Theodore. You know I love you as much as my late Callum, but … Alice?"

"Evoking your Westie, God rest his beautiful, stubborn soul? Whatever is on your mind about Alice and me must be serious." Theodore sighed and sat down. "What about her?" As if he didn't know.

Theodore should have seen it coming. He'd gotten too caught up in Alice. But who could blame him?

Like any man, Theodore spent a lot of time thinking about sex. He'd had his fair share—some rough and fast, other times long and slow. But none of his lovers had ever been so *all in* like Alice. She was fearless once she made up her mind about something—like getting nailed in a supply closet—and it had him pitch caution in the dust bin.

Now, as penance, he'd endure yet another ten-minute lecture from Suzy about his love life. Then he'd find Alice. She was obviously hurt, given how she shuffled out; her beautiful hazel eyes were stunned at learning about her wanker boss. He knew that one was coming, too. But what could he do? He was sworn to secrecy.

Suzy studied him. "Are you playing her?"

"Excuse me?" He loved women and let nature take its course there, but playing someone wasn't in his repertoire. Surely, Suzy knew that after all those years.

She crossed her arms. "I see how she looks at you. It's …"

"What?"

"Familiar. Women fall in love with you, and then …" She cocked her head a little to the right.

"Why don't you just spell it out." They'd known each other for years, so speaking plainly wasn't out of the question.

"You move on, and she's left here." Suzy stepped forward. "She doesn't need the reputation of being the woman who screwed the hot consultant. Oh, yes, I know all about your work breaks with her."

He knew right then he'd made more than a mistake. The two of them having a little fun during the day wasn't his biggest one. Because so, what, truly? Suzy and Samuel weren't prudes. Far from it.

"The only women I meet are through work. And I didn't realize dating someone I worked with was against policy."

"It's not," she said carefully. "Alice is smart, Theo. Don't hurt her."

Pricks broke out across his skin. "You know me better than that. I care about her. A lot."

He'd been thinking a lot about Alice and what she meant to him. How she was different from all the other women he'd been interested in over the years. Even Beatrice.

Suzy arched an eyebrow. "You care?"

"Okay, more than. But with me in a different place every six months, it's not exactly conducive to a steady thing."

"Conducive."

Irritation bubbled up inside him like a volcano. He was

getting tired of her repeating his words. "Yes. Convenient. Propitious. Possible. Pick a word."

"Anything is possible." Her voice was irritatingly calm.

Of course, he knew anything was. But not everything. Having it all wasn't in the cards for anyone. For some reason, he'd thrown that bit of wisdom into the wind when he'd met Alice. She was as ambitious as he was, and honestly, he believed maybe their significant pull to each other would make something work.

But the closer they came to solving the unraveling puzzle of Edison Tech's failure, the closer he came to a trip to the next gig. But doing the long-distance thing? Who was he kidding? He'd tried that with Beatrice and look how that turned out.

"You know there's such a thing as a traveling CFO," Suzy said.

"Oh? You're offering her that? I thought with Roger and his hiding things…" He stopped. He wouldn't be the one to plant a negative idea of Alice in her head. He was, however, a little flummoxed she hadn't caught on to Roger sooner. Her blindness to his moves didn't make sense.

"Roger was clever. He kept her busy as hell in this office. Giving her the office manager and accounting roles in absence of an actual CFO."

"He's a prick and never deserved her."

Suzy's brow furrowed. "What? Tell me she wasn't …."

Shit, that cat leaped from the bag. Suzy didn't know Alice was one of his attempted dalliances.

Suzy shook her head. "My God. Alice with Roger?" She gave off a soft laugh. "I'd have never believed it."

"It's not what you think. Alice was never receptive to Roger's advances." He scrubbed his hair. It didn't remove the image in his head about Roger being near Alice, trying to touch her.

"I see. Well, if she's into you as much as you're clearly into her? Her taste has improved."

Suzy always did know how to slap on the healing salve in the nick of time. "Her taste maybe, but that doesn't mean she'll put up with my schedule."

"Hmm, you may be right. Want to stay here?"

Staying at Edison? He couldn't even imagine what he'd do all day. His skill set required things to be "off." Once they were righted, he moved on.

He shook his head. "Not quitting. Unless you're firing me." He worked damned hard to get where he was. Plus, he rather enjoyed bringing justice to the workplace.

"Wouldn't dream of it. But if you are serious about her, then …" She shrugged and got that look in her eye that told him she had an idea in mind. Whatever it was, he couldn't imagine.

The problem was his imagination wasn't any help, either. They'd committed to exploring each other. See where it led. He never imagined they'd fit so well together or that it'd get so serious so fast. Chemistry, in his experience, generally fizzled out after a month or two. But with Alice, the scent of her, her laughter, and her smart mouth only enflamed his interest like gasoline on a fire.

Dwrn uffern. He more than cared for her. He couldn't get enough of her. And it wasn't because of her spectacular physical assets—she hadn't been wrong about the perfection of her breasts.

It was more the way her face lit up at seeing him, the way she rolled her eyes when he brought up a day to celebrate. It did something inside his chest. He tried to not dwell on it because Suzy had one thing right. He always left town. His job demanded it—the only job that ever fit him.

21

———————

Alice stepped into the elevator. It was only four in the afternoon, but she was cutting out early. She had nine weeks of vacation time saved up. She could take a few hours.

A hand reached out and slapped the door from closing.

Theodore grinned down at her. "Hey. Cutting class?"

Anger radiated through her chest like lightning. His blue eyes glittered as if he hadn't stood in the conference room and lied to her. "Cutting the bullshit." To think she once thought her life made sense. Now? She didn't know what was real anymore.

He hit the down button and wisely kept his mouth shut.

She studied the numbers lighting up, one at a time, as they descended. As each floor passed, her chest grew tighter. Theodore cleared his throat, and the sound grated on her nerves.

She clasped her tongue between her teeth and clenched her fists.

She couldn't hold back. Turning to him, words cascaded out of her like a dam breaking. "How could you? How could *no one* tell me about this sting operation? I was the one who'd been putting up with Roger's BS the last few years. The least anyone could have done was clue me in. I could have helped."

He nodded once.

A slice of fear cut through her anger. "Unless they don't trust me. Or"—she gasped—"suspected me at the beginning and then … Oh, shit, did they think I was in on it?"

His brows furrowed.

She backed up until her back hit the elevator wall. "I would never. My God, and what was that about you were in on it, and—" Her words were lost because he advanced on her, his lips claiming hers.

A soft bounce, and then the elevator was still. The doors whooshed open. Her eyes snapped open and landed on Tricia and Stephanie, who stood in the lobby. Tricia's eyes narrowed, and Stephanie's mouth dropped open. A fan-fuck-ing-tastic addition to that clusterfuck of a day.

Alice pushed Theodore off her. "I almost fell." What a lame thing to say. Especially because they got caught obviously tongue-wrestling each other.

Alice didn't let Tricia or Stephanie say a word. Rather, she bolted out of the elevator, leaving Theodore in the dust.

"Alice," he called.

She kept going. As if running away would change the story Tricia and Stephanie were now surely plotting to spread upstairs?

She could already hear Tricia. *I knew something was up with those two. First Roger and then the hot consultant. She might as well replace her office door with a revolving door.*

And they weren't wrong. She'd screwed Theodore almost everywhere at the office. What had she been thinking?

She wasn't thinking. That was the problem. So much for her dedication to controlling her destiny—and reputation. She spun on him. "Did you have to kiss me?"

"I was trying to make you feel better." He grabbed her hand. "I'll drive you home."

"I can do it." She yanked her hand free.

"Come on. Let me help you."

"No. Did you know he was embezzling? Tell me right now."

Theodore gazed down at her. "Not until a few weeks ago when Samuel brought it up. I wasn't at liberty to tell you."

"A few weeks?" Her shout echoed in the lobby.

The man had been inside her dozens of times. He'd told her he wanted more. Couldn't get enough of her. But he couldn't tell her the truth?

Or maybe the truth was staring her in the face the whole time. Roger set her up. Suzy's questioning all the reports. It was all right there. And Alice was merely collateral—or worse, an unwitting co-conspirator for Theodore's spying— in the O'Flannerys' ultimate plans.

So much for controlling her destiny.

Little pricks formed in her vision. The floor pitched under her feet and then … blessed nothingness.

22

Theodore stared at the woman in his arms. Her couch creaked a little as he adjusted himself. His shirt had grown damp from holding her against his chest as she snoozed.

She snorted. The woman's snores could wake a cemetery. Since napping wasn't in the cards for him, he let his mind drift. Or rather, worry.

His concern for her fainting spells bubbled under his skin. After she woke from her latest spell, he hustled her home, where she quickly fell asleep after they settled on her couch. Perhaps she was exhausted—the kind that snuck up on you, and you didn't realize it until the body just up and quit. She'd certainly lost some weight in the last few weeks. Then again, their lunch hours hadn't exactly been a time for eating.

Suzy's initial question kept coming back to him. *Are you playing her?*

He hadn't been. But then, he hadn't exactly been on the up and up, either. He was trying to protect her. And the more his feelings grew, the more he wanted to tell her everything.

But it was Suzy and Samuel's company. They didn't know

Alice like he did. They didn't assume she'd keep quiet about the investigation, even though she was the most honest person he'd ever met. When the truth came out, he figured Alice would be happy to be rid of Roger, the most *dishonest* person he'd ever met.

One question kept arising, however. How did Alice *not* know about Roger's lies? She was far from naïve.

His phone vibrated on the coffee table for the third time. For God's sake, it was end of day. Enough of both of them working twelve hours a day. He grabbed it with his free hand and hit the button to ignore the call.

She stirred in his arms.

Blinking, she peered up at him. Then, as if recognizing him for the first time, she pushed at his chest and sat up. "I'm mad at you."

"I know." He brushed a lock of hair off her face.

She fell back against him and nestled her face into his neck. "Really mad."

"Yes. But I want you to do something for me."

She scoffed.

"See a doctor. You're fainting too much."

"I have low blood sugar. It's nothing."

"It's not nothing." His phone vibrated again, making an annoying buzz against her wood coffee table. He reached for it to turn the blasted thing off, but the screen's message caught his eye.

A long hiss left his throat. Dammit. "It's Samuel," he explained. In fact, the last five calls had been him.

Alice didn't say anything. Rather, she settled herself cross-legged on the opposite end of the couch.

"Jimmy's Sake Bar. Seven." Samuel's gruff voice filled his ear.

"Not in the mood."

"Get in the mood." Samuel hung up.

God dammit. Suzy must have filled him in on their conversation about Alice. And one thing Samuel did not abide by was romantic messiness at work. Maybe that was why the man had been single for his entire forty-two years. He was as active between the sheets as any man, but no one was allowed to warm them for too long.

He scrubbed his hair and stared down at the floor between his knees. "I've got to go soon."

"Of course you do." Alice's tone was angry but tinged with sadness. "Suzy and Samuel await, right?"

It seemed the entire world was mad at him. Right now, however, only one person mattered in that department: Alice.

His career was important to him. But he'd been alive long enough to know it wasn't everything. Even Suzy and Sammy would have to agree on that point. They didn't spend every holiday together and leave pivotal merger meetings when one landed in a hospital for an emergency appendectomy like Suzy had last year if they didn't believe certain things came first.

He swung his gaze her way. "Samuel. He wants to meet. Come with me?" Why not?

"Not interested. Go ahead and have your discussions without me. As usual."

She had to understand why he couldn't tell her everything. "Alice." He reached for her, but she scrambled to her feet. After wobbling a second, she headed down the hallway to her room.

He heaved out a long sigh and rose. Her bedroom door was locked. He leaned against the hallway wall and slid down to his butt.

"Alice, you can't stay mad at me forever." He hoped.

"Try me." Her voice sounded like she was just on the other side of the door.

"Well, how long is it going to last? Because it's not Be Mad at Everybody Day."

"Enough already."

Maybe it was in poor taste to evoke a day, but he was out of ideas. "Look, I didn't tell you the whole story because I was under a confidentiality agreement. You understand those, right?"

"Questioning my ability to understand contracts and legal documents now, are we?"

"Please open the door so we can talk." He raised his hand and held it against the wood. No more words came from the other side of the door. "It's important you believe I wasn't trying to hurt you."

"Why?"

Good question.

Because I care for you.

Because I've grown addicted to your laugh and the way your lips screw up when I say something stupid about purple golf ball day.

Because I might be in love with you.

The words lodged in his throat.

The reason for his silence was obvious. He was leaving soon, and he wouldn't be the guy Suzy accused him of. Loving and leaving. That was what she was getting at, right? As in, don't tell her you love her and then catch a flight out of there.

It was probably exactly what Suzy believed he was good for. And now Alice might think so as well, and she wouldn't open the door so he could convince her otherwise.

Then again, what could he say? He wasn't moving on to the next company soon? Probably sooner than he thought now that they'd uncovered the real problem with Edison.

But one thing was for sure. He couldn't go like that. He let his hand fall to his thigh. "Alice, please. Be smart about this."

"Go home, Theodore."

He sat there for another five minutes in silence. Home. Where was that anyway?

Finally, he heard some rustling and then the water going on in the shower. He'd been dismissed. It was time to meet Samuel anyway. Likely for his new assignment—or he was truly fired.

23

———————

Theodore slid onto the bar stool. Samuel glanced his way quickly and then back to the guy behind the bar. "Another Nigori."

Theodore waved off the drink suggestion. "I'm good."

"Try it. I can't have this conversation with either one of us fully sober."

"Need an excuse for when you fire me?" He hoped his light tone would belie the possibility of that actually happening.

Samuel's brow furrowed, and he stared at him. "What are you talking about?"

"Suzy fill you in?"

"On?"

"Alice and me." He might as well get to it.

"Oh. That." He went back to studying his sake cup. "Not what I want to talk about."

The man didn't care? Something had changed. Now Theodore was very interested in why he'd been summoned to drink sake on a Tuesday night. "Found out more about Roger?" What else could have the man looking so miserable?

"No. We're cutting him a deal."

"Generous." And futile since the law was the law. Then again, Suzy and Samuel often pulled off the impossible.

Samuel huffed. "Maybe. It can't be more stupid than what I'm about to tell you."

His curiosity was firing on all cylinders now.

The bartender put a white ceramic cup in front of him. "Your Nigori, sir."

What the hell. Theodore picked it up and took a sip that seared his tongue.

Samuel fiddled with his own cup. "What do you know about Patricia Dodd?"

He was so taken aback by Samuel's question his brain had to search for the name's meaning. "Patricia," he stated. "You mean, Patty? At Edison?"

"Programmer. Blonde." He took a sip of his sake. "Fond of pencil skirts."

"Alice's friend." Someone who could keep her mouth shut while he and Alice broke every policy Samuel had about mixing romance with a professional life. Or, in their case, the inability to put their libidos in their rightful place. Or perhaps she did tell, and that was his round-about way of asking if it was true.

"Yeah, that Patty." Samuel continued to play with his cup. "How's Alice, by the way?"

"Mad."

"She should be. Roger was—"

"No. She's mad at me for not filling her in."

"You couldn't have."

"Why not?" He leveled his gaze on Samuel.

Samuel shrugged. "She might have tipped him off. Then again, how did she overlook such a thing? Maybe she was—"

"She'd never." Every word out of Samuel's mouth grew his anger. "Don't you dare think that for one minute. Alice is the best employee you've got at Edison. It was a mistake not letting her in on your suspicions."

Samuel arched an eyebrow. "Is that you talking or your dick?"

Theodore pushed to standing, the bar stool nearly toppling over. "Fuck you, man."

"Sit down, Theodore." He laid his hand on the stool. "I get it. You're in love. For once," he grumbled.

"You don't believe in love."

Samuel smirked. "Know that, do you?"

He remained standing. "Samuel, what's going on?" The man hated to go too deep, so this was a sure-fire way to end it. He didn't have time for Samuel confusing the ever-loving shite out of him—not while a woman he might be in love with wasn't speaking to him. That should be his priority.

Samuel slapped the stool next to him. "Sit down and tell me about Alice. And don't bullshit me."

Something was definitely off with his friend. Theodore took his seat and pushed away the sake cup.

Samuel sighed. "Then tell me what it feels like."

Perhaps something in the sake was turning him crazy. "Feels like?"

"Love." He spat out the word as if it were bitter. "Not sure I'd recognize it."

It took something for Samuel to admit that defect. Suzy and Samuel were used to having all the answers. One thing was clear: Samuel O'Flannery was interested in a woman, and he obviously didn't know what to do about it. Well, that made two of them.

"Not sure I'm the best person to discuss that particular emotion," Theodore said. "Suzy might be better. She'd—"

"Tell me to develop a spreadsheet. Or tell me I'm drinking the same Kool-Aid as you and Alice."

He huffed. "She would do that."

Samuel lifted his sake cup in a toast. "To us confirmed bachelors and the women who drive us crazy."

It stunned him to hear Samuel's assessment of him. Theodore never considered himself committed to staying single. He just took it one day at a time. But he rather enjoyed Samuel's confusion around a woman. It was about time someone drove Samuel to rethink his casual ways.

Theodore lifted his cup and met Samuel's toast before unwisely tipping more sake into his mouth. "You ask Patty out or something?"

"No. She's driving me crazy. From afar. So, tell me. How do you get rid of it? The interest, I mean."

Theodore chuffed. He hadn't a clue about ridding himself of a woman's allure—certainly not Alice's. Only how to unwisely throw himself into her, thinking it'd all sort itself out. "I'll let you know if I ever figure it out."

"You're not trying to stop your interest in Alice, are you?" Samuel studied him under his thick brows.

"No." The answer thunked into his gut. "Can't stay away. So, maybe that's your answer. It feels …"

"Like she's in control?"

Samuel would go there. The man hated being out of control. "No. More like it feels right."

Samuel nodded once, then slapped him on the shoulder. "Then, I say go for it, Theo. I'm sure whatever this … thing is with me will pass. It always does."

Did it? Was that what would happen with Alice eventually? He'd have mulled that over more, except Samuel's tacit approval for Theodore to "go for it" shocked him. Samuel must be truly captivated by Patty to let his long-standing ideas about mixing business with pleasure fall away so easily. It was strange to see Samuel unsure of himself when it came to the opposite sex. Then again, Theodore wasn't in any better boat.

He rose. Time to go see exactly which boat he was in.

He got to Alice's apartment building and gazed up at her bedroom window. It was dark. Her car was parked in its usual spot, however. Was she asleep? Was she ill? He'd make sure she saw a doctor soon.

Leaning against his car, Theodore stared at the email from Suzy on his phone again. The woman was like a river. She flowed one way—forward. He should be thankful. All talk of Alice was gone. Instead, she rambled about their new acquisition, an AI company in Glasgow. The message ended familiarly: "Catch the noon to London tomorrow? We need you on this one."

Need. Such a strange word when one thought about it. What did it mean exactly?

He stared up at Alice's bedroom window again. Would he do the cliched thing of throwing pebbles at it? He looked around at the asphalt parking lot. Not a rock in sight.

He lifted his phone to his ear and prayed she'd answer. She didn't, so he went up anyway.

She answered when he knocked but didn't say a word. Rather, she stood there in a T-shirt and jeans, her big toe making circles on the carpet as she leaned against the door's edge. She wasn't letting him inside yet.

He cleared his throat. "Samuel has a thing for Patty." Her eyes widened and her toe stopped circling. Ah, she didn't know. She certainly hadn't expected to hear those words from him. Hell, he hadn't expected to utter them.

She straightened. "What do you mean? She hasn't said anything to me."

"She probably doesn't know about his interest." Though

he was pretty sure as soon as he left, Alice would call Patty and tell her. "Samuel is good at hiding things."

She scowled. "He's not the only one."

"Ever going to forgive me for adhering to my NDA?"

"You could have suggested to bring me in." She held the door open with one hand. "Did you?"

Now would have been the perfect time to lie about it. Say he did. Try to earn some redemption points, though he wasn't sorry for adhering to the business rules set down by Edison's owners. "Sorry. I've known Suzy and Samuel a long time, and the agreement was set in stone, so …"

"Yeah. I know." She sighed and swung the door open, inviting him in.

"Do you?" He stepped inside. "Do you have any idea how often I wanted to tell you everything?"

Shutting the door, she turned to face him. "So, tell me now."

"How didn't you know about Roger?"

Her eyes narrowed.

Shit. He should have led with something else.

She angrily swiped at hair that had fallen across her forehead. "I just didn't, okay? I was focused on keeping things going. Trying to get that promotion."

"But the books—"

"Are as antiquated as you can get. It was easy for him to skim through altering accounts receivables, unusual company checks, dummy vendors whose agreements I never signed! You want to be believed, then you need to believe me. It's how it works."

He did trust her. "Fair enough."

"Good. Now, don't ever lie to me again. Or leave out anything important."

The relief that she was granting him some grace for

keeping the full truth of his presence at Edison washed over him like a waterfall. "Then let's talk."

He then proceeded to tell her everything. He confessed it all, like how he was brought in to ferret out anything at all that was remiss at Edison. Personnel was his mission, but Suzy and Samuel had admitted they suspected financial fraud. They'd suspected Alice was in on it. He hurt her deeply with that bit of information. But she'd said to not hold anything back.

He grasped her hand. "I didn't believe it from the second I met you."

"Oh?" Pain still swam in her eyes.

"You're loyal."

She scoffed. "Stupidly so."

"No." He held her hand for long minutes. Finally, given it was after midnight, he rose, pulling her up. "Time to sleep." The time for talk was over. Plus, he didn't want to leave room for discussion about Samuel's strange interest in Patty. Or that he learned the future of Edison Tech was in danger. He also didn't want to go into the growing ache in his chest that he couldn't tell if it was love or not. And most of all, he wasn't ready to share the fact he had to get on a plane soon— without her.

For the first time, they shared a bed and didn't have sex. Perhaps they were too tired from the day. But it felt … odd. Maybe the bubble was finally bursting. Just when he'd been given permission from his bosses to go for it.

Life could be a cruel beast.

24

Roger hovered in Alice's office doorway, a security guard dressed in all black behind him about fifteen feet away. She was honestly shocked to see both of them.

Roger cleared his throat. "I suppose you heard."

"I did." She returned to look at her computer screen, unsure of what to say. Sorry? How could you? Could you have been any more idiotic?

Then again, maybe she was the idiot. She hadn't noticed what he'd been up to. She'd been kept in the dark not only by the company's owners but by the man she'd been sleeping with—a man she concluded last night she should have *never* slept with so soon. It clouded her judgment. As Theodore had said, she was trusting—too much, too soon.

"I'm stepping down, effective immediately," Roger said. "But I wanted to say goodbye."

It took effort to keep her eyes on her screen. "Goodbye, Roger."

"I'll miss you."

That made her look up. "Don't."

"We could have been good together. I wish things had turned out differently."

A completely uncalled-for laugh rose up her throat. "Good? We were never together, Roger."

He stepped farther in, causing her to jump up. He looked visibly taken aback that she'd startled so badly. He showed her both of his palms. "Alice, you've got to believe me. I never meant to—"

"To what? Steal? You should have thought of that before."

His face hardened. "You're a smart woman. Surely you don't think I—"

"What? That you embezzled? I saw the evidence with my own eyes."

Then it hit her. He dangled a promotion to keep her malleable. Quiet. "You were never going to make me CFO, were you?"

He cleared his throat. "You're young. You have time—"

"Time?" How she put up with him for so long, she'd never know. "Yeah. I have that. But you don't."

His face purpled. "This office will be lost without me."

"Oh, really? I'd say this office is feeling better. You know Theodore—"

"Who you're fucking."

Her belly dropped to her knees. "Excuse me?" she spluttered. Her face turned into a human sunset, which only added to her humiliation.

"I know all about it."

A sliver of defiance rose inside her. "From whom?"

"How about everyone?"

"Oh, really?" Her voice had risen, and the security guard shifted on his feet in the background.

Roger tsked. "As smart as you are, you're easily fooled."

"No, I'm not." Except Roger had fooled her, hadn't he? Changing up the books? She'd utterly failed at her one job.

"Then why are you with a guy who flits from office to office, all managed by the O'Flannerys, of course, leaving a trail of broken hearts?"

"He flirts with everyone."

"And sleeps with them, too."

Alice wasn't naïve enough to think he didn't have liaisons now and again. He was a guy. Was everyone supposed to believe he'd be celibate? But then a part of her—probably the smart part everyone kept referencing—spoke up. He was a flirt and probably did have his trysts. But before or after his fiancée dumped him for his best friend? Only one thing she knew for sure. He moved on to the next gig and didn't take anyone with him.

She closed her eyes for one long second, then snapped them open "So? It doesn't matter what he did in the past." The lie felt like a burn on her tongue. But she wouldn't let Roger see the way his words impacted her.

"It's not in the past. It's happening right now. With you."

His words fit inside her, like interlocking pieces meant for only her. They felt like the truth.

Gah. Had she been so blind? Been the candidate for Miss December with Roger and Miss January with a different guy? She refused to believe it. She was still mad at him, but she honestly believed Theodore had good intentions.

Roger stepped forward. "I have it on good authority that Theodore does this everywhere he goes. I've known the O'Flannerys a while, too." He'd softened his tone, as if trying to console her. He reached his arm out, and she recoiled.

Roger sighed heavily and dropped his arm. "He charms. Seduces. Acts chivalrous."

Jesus. Her thoughts exactly. Except she believed it was all for her. "You're wrong about him." She would defend Theodore until he gave her reason to not. Theodore was a good consultant. She'd seen how he got people to open up and talk. She also admired how he not only did his job, but he had fun, too.

"I'm not."

The security guard was closer now. "Sir? Time to go."

Alice crossed her arms over her chest. "Have a nice life, Roger." She pushed past him and marched to Theodore's office. Roger was trying to make her paranoid. She was having none of it.

Upon her entrance, Theodore lifted his gaze from whatever he was peering at on his desk.

He grinned widely at her. "Just in time for lunch. *Outside.*"

"No time." She raised her hand. "Not today. Just had a little chat with Roger."

His face steeled. "Need me to kick him out for you?"

"No. He's being escorted out as we speak." She closed his door and turned to face him. "I need to know something. About your time at the other O'Flannery companies." She wouldn't stew about it. In fact, she'd never again hold back a question that needed asking. She and mystery were no longer on speaking terms.

"We talked about that last night. No one's embezzled as far as I've heard. Suzy would have their balls on a stick. In fact, Roger has no idea how lucky he is."

"*No.*" She shook her head. "Do you do this …" She waved her hand between them. "Get a new girlfriend at every one of your gigs and then move on?"

"You still don't trust me." His mouth set in a grim line.

"I don't know you that well." It was true.

A muscle in his jaw ticked. "Well enough, I'd say. At least enough to not accuse me of something you keep making up in your head. That's what's going on, isn't it? God." He shook his head. "You sound like Beatrice."

The nerve. "There's more to that story, isn't there? What happened?"

His face turned to stone. The usual twinkle in his eyes extinguished. "I'm not talking to you about her."

Fair enough. She was heading down a rabbit hole, and his past relationships weren't her business. But she had reasons to be suspicious. "I'm not making up anything."

Except she had.

She'd made up she and Theodore having a future. Shit. That little truth landed in her gut like an anvil. She'd believed there was National BAE Day waiting for her in June. "Tell me, once you're relieved of your duties here, where to next?"

He lifted one shoulder. "Back to London for a spell. Then, Suzy mentioned a fresh start in some AI generation—"

"Do you love me?" Her breath stalled in her throat. The question couldn't be held back any longer. Perhaps it'd been sitting there for weeks, souring until she had to spit it out.

He shuffled on his feet. His lips parted to speak but then closed as if no words came to him. Certainly not a yes.

She nodded slowly, and her eyes still stupidly pricked. "It's okay. Really." Or it would be once she had time to think about how to unravel the emotional minefield she'd landed in.

The ice in his eyes melted a bit. He quickly rounded his desk and took both of her hands. "Yes."

He yanked her into him. All she could focus on was his blue eyes, and the growing warmth in them. Their lips met halfway. The kiss wasn't gentle. Lips, tongues digging in deep as if they were trying to dissolve the distance between them. Noisy breaths came through his nose, and his hands clutched at her back, keeping her tight against him. She loved being swallowed by his body, his mouth.

She'd vowed to keep a little anger tucked away inside for him keeping her in the dark for so long. Yeah, that pledge melted to nothing under the force of his kiss.

When they finally broke apart, he kept his forehead against hers.

"You love me." Her voice was barely above a whisper.

"Yes. But …"

The worst word in the English language after I love you was "but." She swallowed and lifted her head to take in his beautiful eyes.

His hold loosened, and he stepped backward. "My job here is done. I leave tomorrow."

Her heart panged painfully. "Tomorrow. So soon?"

"Yes. It's …" He let his words trail off.

She was a big girl. She could take the turn of events. "Well, damn. Just when I took your advice and made a doctor's appointment."

He gave her a half smile. "Good. You'll call me and tell me what he says?"

Not discuss it over real tea in person or have him tell her when it was National Fainting Day. That was when her heart nearly split in two. He knew it had to be over, too, didn't he?

"What *she* says. And yes. I'll … call." Because he wouldn't be there.

"Hey." He tucked a piece of hair behind her ear. "Want to get out of here? I don't have much to pack, and tonight, we could …"

He let his words trail off. They could what? Act like it was an ordinary night? Indulge in each other one last time? Talk about having text sex in some lame attempt to close the distance between them? He loved her, but what did that mean? What kind of future could they possibly have together? Weekly video calls? Sexting sessions? The occasional weekend?

Still, she nodded and tried very hard not to think about how it was the last time he'd walk across Edison's lobby to the parking lot. She grabbed her purse, followed him out, neither of them talking or touching.

No one interrupted their slow walk to the elevator, though plenty of people stared. Could they tell? Could they see the blanket of sadness draped over her?

As soon as they were in the elevator, he grasped her hand. "Do you need to get anything from home?"

"Home?"

"I want us to go to my place tonight."

"No, I don't need anything." Except you, she wanted to shout.

He nodded once, and the elevator lurched downward. And for the first time, she understood the saying that sometimes love wasn't enough.

With one click of Theodore's condo door, the air seemed to constrict. She'd followed him to his rental, a place she'd only seen once.

"Haven't had a chance to clean up," he said with a half laugh.

She glanced around. The condo was basic, with a couch, chairs, TV on the wall, and a small kitchen to the left. Nothing too personal, nothing to suggest anyone spent much time there. "If this is messy, then how on earth did you stay at my place?" She tried to laugh, but a scoff came out instead.

"You were there. That's all that mattered."

Heat climbed up her neck.

He drew closer, and she closed the space between them as if they were two magnets. It was always like that with him. The closer he got, the more she needed to be near him.

With a soft moan, Theodore lifted her up by the ass. She starfished herself against him, wrapping her legs around his waist and her arms around his broad shoulders. Once again, she felt his strength, his size. Her stupid eyes pricked, and she choked down emotion that lodged in her throat.

He walked them down a short hallway to his bedroom. Instead of laying her down on the bed, he sat, keeping her in his lap. His eyes stayed trained on her face as he pulled her shirt out of her skirt.

His palms moved to inch under her blouse. "I need to feel your skin." His lids hooded when his fingers met her bare back. Little sparks of electricity ignited under his touch.

A long breath escaped her lips as his cock pressed between her legs. She'd never have a man fit her so well.

"We can elevate our sexting to video," he said. "Or have a regular weekend where we meet somewhere."

"A regular weekend. Yeah."

"You'd love London."

"I would." She couldn't care less. "Where's the AI company you're going to next?"

"Glasgow."

"Oh. Far." It didn't matter where he was. It wouldn't be DC, where she was. She pushed his jacket off his shoulders. "I need to feel you, too."

He rose and deposited her on the bed. Keeping his eyes on her the entire time, he undid his belt and his pants and lowered them, taking his boxer briefs with him. His thick cock sprung forward, and the ache between her legs built into a small fire.

"You lick your lips like that one more time, I'll lose it right here," he said as he crawled over her, pushed her down. "And I plan on spending a very long time inside you."

The way he stared at her, there was no question he wanted her. But there was more there. He'd said she was *more than* more than a fling. It was in his kiss, the way his hands roamed her body with such intention as if he sought to memorize her.

She captured her bottom lip with her teeth. "That's one way to miss your plane."

He shoved his hips between her legs, and they made way for him. "There'd just be another one I'd have to catch."

Stupid tears formed in her eyes. His eyes blazed, his hands cradled her head. "Hey, it's not forever."

"I know," she squeaked. "But—"

His lips found hers, and any words she might have spoken were swallowed.

Theodore took his time with her, pressing kisses along her neck. She thought he murmured something—my BAE? At least that was what she thought he'd whispered. She could have imagined it.

His hips started to rock into her with more urgency, and she met him halfway. Her hands clawed at his back, but no matter how hard she tried, she couldn't get him close enough.

It was only later, when he fell asleep and she lay in the dark staring up at his hideous popcorn ceiling that something dawned on her. He didn't once bring up a special holiday today.

Alice stared at the flight app. Theodore's flight had departed on time. She didn't go to the airport with him because no way would she devolve into a crying cliché in front of hundreds of people.

Not that she'd have missed anything at Edison. Nothing was getting done. She'd stared at the same financial report for the last hour, not taking in any of the figures.

Tea. That was what she needed. Funny how she'd slowly morphed into a tea drinker over the last few weeks.

The kitchen was quiet. A calm had entered the air. Very much like a morgue.

She popped in a Twinings pod and had to choke back the lump that formed in her throat.

"Ah, Alice." Suzy appeared in the doorway. "I wanted you to hear this from me directly. We're seeking a buyer for Edison. More likely than not, though, we won't find one. In that case, we're shuttering."

Oh. Her plans were real if she was risking telling Alice that in the hallway. But funny how not an ounce of fear arose at the news. Alice truly was over being there, wasn't she? "Sounds like a plan."

"You held this place together. It was noticed."

"I don't want to hold things together anymore." In fact, at that second, a burning desire to quit arose. But what would she do?

Suzy stepped inside the kitchen. "You have choices, Alice. You're free to do what you want, of course. Or you can become CFO of one of our other companies."

"Oh?" She couldn't muster any enthusiasm for the deal. My, how times had changed. If Suzy had offered her that even last week, she'd have had trouble staying inside her skin.

Suzy arched a perfect brow. "Neither of those appeal?"

"It's … I don't know. I'm …" She couldn't get the words out. It would be humiliating to admit she was a big ball of feelings. She was pretty sure Suzy O'Flannery never once wanted to crawl into bed with a plate of brownies and never leave like Alice did at that moment. Could Alice get any more cliched?

Suzy closed the door, which snapped Alice to attention. Leaning against the door, she crossed her arms over her chest. "You're upset."

"No, I'm fine."

"Good. Then there's a third option." Suzy stepped so close Alice could make out a little smudge of mascara under one of her eyes.

"A third?"

"I have an idea I want to discuss with you. Something I've been thinking about for some time. It'd be lucrative for you —and us. Ready to hear it?"

Alice put her cup down on the small table and took a seat. After all, she didn't have anywhere else to go.

Suzy took the opposite seat. "Theodore is good with

people; so are you. But differently. He gets people to talk. You solve their problems, which means you're good at ferreting them out. It's amazing what small things keep people from being productive."

"I'm just … handy."

"Oh, you're more than that. You understand how everything impacts our bottom line. I understand from Theodore you had quite a few ideas to increase our profitability. I'd like to hear them, even if Edison can't be saved. Would you be willing to go on the road for us as a consultant? Like Theodore."

"No," she said quickly, surprising even herself.

Suzy leaned back and assessed her. "I didn't take you for a quitter."

"What? Not wanting to be horseshoed into—"

"Is that you think it is? I believe together you'd uncover all manners of ills that need to be addressed. I'm thinking you'll start at"—she looked at her thoughtfully—"two hundred thousand?"

Was the woman crazy? "T-two hundred *thousand?*"

"As a start. You and Theodore will have matching salaries. I expect we'll make up for that the first month you're out."

Out? She and Theodore might never be in the same time zone again. She stared down at the ugly industrial carpeting, not quite wanting to see the disappointment in Suzy's eyes. Not wanting to admit why her offer didn't appeal.

"There's a reason, isn't there?" Suzy finally asked. Her tone was gentle—like nothing she'd ever heard from the woman. Suzy sucked in a long breath, let it out. "You know, I never married."

Alice snapped her gaze back up. "I-I know." Everyone did, given how much publicity she'd gotten.

"It was my choice, and the right one for me, though I do have my moments of doubt."

She couldn't imagine Suzy doubting herself in any decision. "Oh." She honestly didn't have a single better word to say to the odd admission—and even stranger confession.

"I don't want to lose you, Alice. Tell me." She rose and perched one hip on the table. "Is there a personal reason you don't want to consider this? You're not obligated to tell me anything, of course, but—"

"Yes. There is." A sharp stab went through her heart. Even if Theodore got on a plane that morning, a small part of her still hoped they'd figure something out.

She'd arrived at Edison that morning, stepped off the elevator, and headed to her office like she had a thousand times. But it wasn't the same anymore. She wanted something *more*.

Suzy smiled at her. "I thought so. You want room for a personal life." She dipped her chin and peered at her. "With a certain red-headed Welsh gentleman, perhaps?"

Alice nodded slowly. "But it's impossible."

Suzy scoffed immediately. "Nothing is impossible. But I won't lose Theodore." She eyed Alice. "You know, I have another idea. If Theodore has shown me anything—and don't look so surprised, I'm still learning, too—is that happy people are more productive. So." She stood. "Go on the road with him."

"What?"

"Become a two-person team." She shrugged like it was the easiest thing to do in the world. "From what Samuel tells me, Theodore's not going to be his best self if I cut you off from him. And I refuse to have productivity dip."

"That would be bad," she agreed, though not quite understanding how she and Theodore could work together.

"We're on the same page, then. Have you ever been to Glasgow?"

"No." Her head began to spin. Suzy was serious.

"I prefer Edinburgh myself. But we have a start-up we might acquire. I think you'll start there. Then, later, Australia—"

"Australia?" Her eyes widened, and she was having trouble taking in a full breath.

"You'll fly international business class, of course."

"Oh. Good." Good? Suzy was laying out her whole future as if it were a done deal. But if there was one thing she learned during the last weeks, she couldn't control everything, but she could pick and choose her battles. She had to have boundaries of her own making. "But what if it's not a good fit?"

"Oh, I think Theodore *fits* you well."

Did Suzy make a sexual innuendo? Alice swallowed. As if that would tamp down her body's reaction to even thinking about being with Theodore *fitting*?

"What does Theodore think?" Surely, Suzy had run the idea of teaming up with someone by him.

"I've never suggested it. But I'm positive he believes you're a perfect fit, too." She took in a quick breath. "Now, go see him. Go home and pack. There's a day flight to London, but you'll need to hurry. It leaves at noon. Use the company credit card—business class. I'll have a car at your place to take you to the airport."

"London?"

Suzy sighed as if Alice wasn't catching on quick enough for her taste. "Yes, Alice. Go to Theodore. Tell him what I said. I want you both to discuss this without my influence."

"This is moving really fast. I mean, what if it can't work?"

Suzy rose and smiled down at her. "You want to know the secret to success in business?" She didn't wait for an answer. "It isn't just what you choose. It's knowing there's always more than one answer. Or in this case, two. It's not an either-

or Alice. It's a … Make Your Own Way Day." She winked at her.

But London? Get on a plane. Be with Theodore. Work with Theodore. Be on the road? Her head was swimming. But one thing was for sure, a sliver of excitement took hold. Maybe if she took the opportunity as an exploratory thing. She could always talk to him, see what he said, then decide. Even start consulting with him, and if it didn't work …

"You're thinking too much, Alice."

A smile finally appeared on Alice's face. "I do have a lot of vacation saved up."

"Granted. But be back soonish? You're valuable to us as we shut things down."

Valuable. She now understood what that meant. Suzy needed her and was willing to reward her for it. Alice rose and held out her hand. "Thank you."

"Don't thank me yet." Suzy clasped both of her hands around Alice's. "I expect a lot from my employees. Either as a management consultant or as my CFO of O'Flannery Enterprises."

Her lips dropped open. "You mean both are on the table?"

"If you want it."

"But I didn't—"

"Catch Roger?" She scoffed, dropping her hand hold. "It took us nine months to figure it out. Suffice to say, you keeping this place going during it was enough. Now, go. Airports are hell these days. Not that I ever spend any time in them anymore."

The woman really did have a private jet, didn't she? One day, Alice promised herself, she'd have the option for one. Not that money was important. Right then. Only one thing was. And he had the bluest eyes she'd ever seen.

Before Suzy could scoot out, Alice had one more pressing

matter. "What about the others? Patty Dodd is the best programmer I've ever seen. And Harrison and …"

She held up her hand. "Generous packages to all. Though I might have to steal Patty back. She's good."

"The best."

"And a best friend, I presume. She never let on about you and Theodore."

Shit. Suzy had eyes in the back of her head—or ESP.

Before Alice could respond, Suzy leaned closer and dropped her voice. "When you do start working together …" She already thought it was a done deal? "Keep the supply closet visits down to one a day?" She winked again at Alice.

Even through a blush with the strength of the sun, she looked at Suzy directly. "I can do that." *Maybe.*

But first, she had to find out if Theodore was interested in sharing a clothes closet at home and not just a supply closet. Not only be a management consulting team. No way could she work with him if BAE Day wasn't real. She'd crossed a line. She loved him. She couldn't downgrade to mere colleagues. It was impossible.

As Theodore stepped out of the clipper boat's seating area, the cold February air slapped him in the face. He'd have to rethink his love of that season. In fact, he might write off winter altogether. Too many memories.

Completing a project usually invigorated him. Moving on to the next project even more. Now, it was as if he were sleepwalking.

He strode down the street away from the pier, swinging his little bag of tea he'd secured at the Borough Market. Not even finding his favorite Darjeeling blend in stock at the tiny stall could lift his mood. At least the venture had eaten up some time and helped clear the growing fog in his head.

As he waited for the street's crossing to be clear, a gust of wind cut through his jacket, sending a chill up his spine. The sky was gray. Rain threatened, as usual. It normally didn't bother him. London had always felt like home to him. Except everything seemed flatter, less vibrant than he recalled. He felt it the second he'd landed a few days ago.

He glanced once more at his phone screen. Not a single return message from Alice. He'd pinged her as soon as his plane had touched down on the tarmac. Then again when he got to his flat. Then another late last night and a fourth that morning.

All night, his mind bounced back and forth between whether or not to grab a plane back to the States. Why not make America homebase and stay close to Alice? Suzy and Samuel could see to it. But there was the little fact that he'd still be gone as much as ever, which squashed that idea.

He supposed he could get a job elsewhere or even find something else to do at the O'Flannery companies, something that would tether him to one place. The trouble was, there were no other O'Flannery companies outside of Edison in DC, so he'd be chained to an office far away from her.

God. A vision of him sitting at a desk, an unknown skyline out his window, rose in his mind, making his stomach curdle. He'd be bored to death. Perhaps Beatrice's parting words to him were true after all. *You're married to the airport.*

Being away from Alice, however, felt wrong.

He sucked in a lungful of cold air and picked up the pace just as white flakes began to float from the sky. Unusual for London. People began to pause all around him to lift their faces to the sky.

An old woman in a brown wool coat standing near him smiled at him. "It's snowing."

"That it is." He lifted his hand. It was a marvel. Snow didn't fall often in the city. Alice should see it. An instant pang in his chest made his shoulders hunch forward.

He picked up the pace, letting the flakes swirl around him. As soon as he turned onto his street, though, his feet stopped moving. A figure huddled close by his building's door. It was a woman. White dusted her hair.

His breath caught in his throat. "Alice," he called.

She turned, her cheeks a bright pink and her hands stuffed under her armpits. He jogged to her.

Her teeth chattered. "I thought it never snowed here." She wasn't wearing gloves or a hat, which made him chuckle a little. For a woman who thought of everything—usually—the weather continued to get by her.

He placed one foot on the first step. "How did you find me?"

"Suzy told me where you lived. I don't suppose we can go inside?" She stomped her feet a little. She wore little ballerina slippers with no socks, of course. At least they weren't heels.

Why was he delaying? He jogged up the stairs and scooped her into his arms. "I thought you said you had wellies."

"They're back in DC because the weather app didn't warn me."

With one arm around her, he fished in his jeans for his keys. "At least you checked it this time."

He let them in, and she followed him up the one flight of rickety stairs to his flat. Thank God the cleaners had been there the other day.

As soon as they stepped inside, blessed warmth enveloped him. Alice blew on her fingers.

He got his boots off and hung his coat. Then he took hers. As soon as he touched it, her scent filled the space.

He drew closer to her again and rubbed her arms, marveling at the fact that he could touch her again. "You're cold. Let me make you some tea."

"That would be good," she breathed out.

"Sit." He pointed to his small sofa.

She sat down and immediately glanced around. "So, this is where you live."

"It is."

She waved her hand toward him. "I don't think I've ever seen you out of a suit."

"Hmm. I believe I've shed quite a few around you."

She flushed a bright red. "I mean, the jeans. Looks good." Her fingers twisted together, and she chewed on her lip. She jumped up again. "I think I'll move around a bit. I was sitting for a long time." Her nerves were on full display as she began to pace, her eyes darting to the floor as if thinking.

"So, about that tea. I have this marvelous Darjeeling—"

"Anything is fine." She waved her hand.

"I'll bring it to you," he said cautiously.

"I can help." She moved to follow him and bumped against him. A jolt of static electricity ran up his back.

She gasped. "Oh, sorry."

What was up with her? The fact that she flew all that way to see him was a surprise, but her jumpiness was unexpected. He spun on her and pulled her closer. "What's wrong?"

"Nothing," she said in too high of a pitch voice. "Suzy's closing Edison."

He wasn't shocked, though no one had alerted him of the plans. But her sudden presence made sense. "You were let go?"

"No. I was given options. That's why I'm here, actually. It's Make Your Own Way Day." She plastered on a fake smile.

"Hate to break it to you, but there's no such day I'm aware of."

Her usual fire returned to her eyes. "Know everything, do you?"

"Clearly not. I didn't know you were coming."

Her lips fell open. "Wish I didn't?"

"Of course, I'm glad you're here. It's just, other than tea, I've got nothing in the larder, and—"

"Theodore, I'm asking you right now. Tell me to leave, and I'll never bother you again."

She was worried he was unhappy to see her. "Why would I do that? I meant it when I said I loved you." He pulled her into a hug. "Now, what's got you so nervous?"

She made herself still, looked him directly in his beautiful eyes. "Suzy thinks we should work together. Co-management consultants, traveling around together, which would mean we would see a lot of each other, though she said we had to keep the supply closet visits down to one a day, which, of course, I agreed to, but I'm not sure you would be or were even thinking that way, so I'm here to ask you—"

"Once a day? Forget it."

She blinked like she hadn't quite heard him right. "Oh, I see." She stepped backward. "Of course, if you don't want—"

"No." He grasped her, pulled her back to him. "You misunderstand. There is no way in hell I could be near you and not want to live in the supply closet." His gaze raked her from head to toe. Granted, she'd stepped off an airplane recently and was dressed completely and utterly wrong in little soaked ballerina flats, black trousers, and a blouse underneath a leather jacket, of all things. But the desire to strip her nude, lay her down right on the hardwood floor, and make her scream out his name rose strong.

Then he wanted to make her a proper lunch and make sure she got to bed at a decent hour.

He wanted to show her around London. Take her to the Sky Garden where she could see the whole of the city from its rooftop garden.

Take her to the Twinings Tea Museum and show her what proper tea looked, smelled, and tasted like.

Then, there was Skomer Island, Bannau Brycheiniog, and Cornwall to visit.

Jesus, he'd mapped out their life in a nanosecond.

He took both her hands in his. "I've spent all night trying to figure out how to get back to America—"

"You did?" she asked quickly.

"Yes, but the truth is, I won't be happy there. And I get your job is important to you, so …"

A smile cracked across her face. "Not exactly. Talking to Suzy clarified something for me. It isn't my job so much as my *career*. What I *do* all day. What I've been doing at Edison was a dead end. Even if I made CFO there, it's small potatoes. You were right about one thing. I did too much that wasn't helping me in that job. But Suzy thinks I'd be great at helping ferret out problems. So, care to hear what she proposed?"

He eyed her. "I'm listening." With a healthy dose of interest. He'd worked for Suzy and Samuel long enough to know they never made offers that weren't serious.

She moved to her big bag, which she'd abandoned by the front door. After rustling around in it, she pulled out a manilla folder. "You would continue to do what you do."

"Celebrate Breast Appreciation Day?" He held up his hands. "Not making it up. January second."

She laughed and slapped his chest with her folder. "Be serious. You get people to talk, open up. I watch for other problems."

"Like embezzlement."

"I'm giving you a pass on that one." She pointed at him. "But only one. I'm the perfect person to catch anything like that because *never again*. I'm talking about the day-to-day inefficiencies, the things that slow people's production. Stuff like that."

"And another one falls." He slapped his chest, hung his head. "The corporate vague speak is the first sign."

An exasperated sigh left her mouth. "Look"—she opened her folder—"I did the spreadsheet on the pros and cons. And do not let this go to your head, but partnering with you came out on top of all three opportunities I have."

He must have looked clueless because she rolled her eyes.

"Suzy said I could leave altogether and find another job or become CFO of O'Flannery Associates—"

"Whoa. That's huge."

She beamed him a smile. "Right? Or my third option is to partner with you."

He was sure Alice had no idea the crown Suzy had placed on her beautiful head. Suzy O'Flannery didn't meet someone and offer them a C-suite position often. She groomed them. Made them toil at one of her companies before considering them to be part of the parent organization.

Then again, Alice was special. Jesus, he never wanted to leave her again.

"I don't know." He pointed at her spreadsheet. "My knowing Breast Appreciation Day is not on here, so I'm not sure it was a fair calculation. I could have scored higher here. You know how I worship your assets."

Alice crossed her arms. "Fine, I'll go to Australia by myself."

He blinked at her, not quite sure what she was talking about.

She sighed heavily. "You really need to keep up. First, we'd need to do that AI company in Glasgow, then there's a start-up in Australia Suzy wants us on. So, if you don't want to …" She studied her manicure as if she didn't have time for the conversation.

"The BSY Group? No way are you doing that without me." One whiff of power and the woman was already trying to lead things. He actually didn't mind.

She was adorable when she set her sights on something. All that fire in her eyes, her impatience with him when he didn't read her mind. It could be fun to form a team with her, set a rhythm, and adopt some cues that only they knew about. Like what Suzy and Samuel had.

"So, you're in?" she asked.

Rarely did anyone move faster than he did. Certainly, he'd never pictured Alice taking such leaps.

He hadn't imagined being on the road with Alice as a possibility. Sharing a hotel room or a rental apartment with Alice. Like they were a real couple. Only she had no idea what rarely being home was really like.

He scratched his head. "Business travel isn't like vacation or making a home. It's constantly living in the 'in between'."

"Worried I'll cramp your style?" she asked.

"No." She was getting all the wrong ideas. "I'm worried about you."

"Why? Oh ..." she drew out. "My doctor said what I thought. Low blood sugar. I have to eat protein every four to six hours. What a pain—and hard."

"Not if you have someone watching out for you. A partner who makes you stop for lunch."

"With iced tea?"

"Forget it. Now, why didn't Suzy tell me about this?" He'd also read Samuel the riot act for not filling him in. Those two never made offers like that without consulting one another. And he rather enjoyed being part of their inner circle.

"She respects you too much. She wanted us to discuss it without her influence. For us to determine whether we ... fit."

Oh, they fit, all right. Even if she had no taste in tea. But he appreciated the nod Alice gave to him about Suzy and Samuel respecting him.

"Well, I don't know," he said. "Is this a corporate team with benefits? Because if it's not, I'm not sure I can watch you bend over in those skirts and solve problems at the same time without some supply closet promises."

Now, she was really smiling. "I wouldn't have it any other way."

Being on the road with Alice. Now that the possibility

arose, he honestly couldn't imagine living alone in a rented flat or hotel suite without her ever again.

He yanked her closer and engulfed her in his arms. "And you have to promise me you'll kiss me all day on Kiss a Ginger Day."

"Only if you promise me National BAE Day. I also want Breast Appreciation Day and other holidays as I discover them. To be determined."

God, he loved that woman. Truly, deeply, *for real* love.

"Deal." His mouth crashed down on hers. For long minutes, their tongues tangled as he breathed in her scent and let his hands roam every inch of her he could reach.

Alice. Alice. Alice. Her name kept ringing in his head as he worked over her lips. His hands couldn't stop themselves. He lifted her up, and God love her, she wrapped her legs around his waist.

He carried her to his bedroom. The tea could wait. Hell, the whole world could wait.

Through his bedroom window, the snow falling from the sky had picked up. It was really coming down, blanketing everything in white. Right then, winter moved back to his favorite season spot.

As soon as her back hit the bed, their kiss broke. Her dark eyes gazed up at him. "I love you, Theodore Gaston the Fourth."

"And I love you, Alice. I will forever."

Her glorious lips glistened in the low light. "You just won first place in my spreadsheet."

Every part of his body buzzed with happiness. "I'd say I won. I get to be your Before Anyone Else. *Jackpot.*"

"And you are mine. Now, kiss me again, ginger."

It was the next morning before any thought of tea crossed their minds.

EPILOGUE

June 10

Alice shivered, despite Theodore's warm hand tugging her along the sidewalk. So much for National BAE Day being sunshine and roses. It'd been gray, drizzly and miserable all weekend despite the fact that it was June.

Still, she wouldn't let the near-constant London rain ruin their day, their first real anniversary-type date. It had to be perfect.

Her fingers found the small gray box from Clairmont Diamonds in her raincoat pocket. It held the wedding band she'd picked out for Theodore. It was a simple platinum band with their initials and a scrolled inscription inside. Over tea in the fanciest place she could find, the Lanesborough Hotel, she would propose to him.

She'd spent weeks setting it up. First, begging for a reservation on June 10—National BAE Day. She told the woman who answered the phone about how they first met and the deal they made and then broke and then made again.

The woman had laughed and told her she could sneak in two more people that day. Alice even sprung to reserve the best bottle of champagne they offered.

"We need to be in Kensington by 3 pm," she'd told Theodore that morning. "It's a surprise."

"That's perfect," he'd said. "I have a surprise for you, too. But, first let's take a walk."

Ah, Londoners' favorite pastime, she'd learned. They walked everywhere. But a team of wild horses had taken up residence in her belly, so a stroll did sound good to calm some of those beasts down a bit. She tended to blurt things out when nervous, and she was determined to keep everything secret until the big moment.

She had today all planned.

After they sat down to high tea, and it was poured, she'd lift her cup and propose a toast.

Her whole speech had been written and rewritten and she finally settled on something simple. "You're the best man I've ever met. And I want us to be together forever. Would you be willing to be my husband?"

He'd then say "yes," of course, and she'd slide the little box to him.

It was unorthodox for the woman to be asking the question and presenting him with a ring. But it felt right to her.

She'd discovered over the last few months how good Theodore was for her. How she could be both in control and spontaneous at once. It was remarkable, really.

Then there was the fact that they made an effective team in the companies they visited. True to Suzy's word, Theodore was good at getting people to talk. Alice, on the other hand, truly had a knack for uncovering what made people unproductive.

Like the AI company in Glasgow. Everyone was so enamored with the possibilities and profits, they didn't even think about their expenses. An unlimited budget meant an office kitchen that rivaled an *Architectural Digest* spread with an espresso machine, catered lunches and more. That meant people hung out for long lunches—and their workday was reduced by 17 percent. Suzy seemed to love that Alice nailed that one.

Then, there was the company in Cleveland who didn't invest in their employees at all, including not providing parking. So everyone spent at least 6 percent of their day walking from wherever they could leave their car to the office. Or, worse, commuted by train which wasn't even near the office. That was a 14 percent reduction in productivity.

At both companies, Theodore got to the heart of their employees' complaints. Then Alice put numbers to it, which caused their CFOs to instantly change things.

But more than that, Theodore had proved to be fun. Weights she didn't know she'd been living with had lifted from her shoulders by his presence. Things just went right around him.

Like the time the fire alarm kept going off all night in that terrible hotel in Nashville. Every time they went out, he led a sing-along of "Burning Down the House" by Talking Heads with the other pajama-clad guests right on the street.

Turned out he was a great cook, showing her how to make protein-rich vegetarian balls with almond butter, coconut, oatmeal and protein powder that she could stash in her purse for long meetings.

And when they were back in London, his flat was so small they kept bumping into each other which invariably led into all kinds of sexy times. She could sit on his bathroom sink and have her feet propped on the opposite wall while he pitched into her. She never wanted a too-large house again.

Theodore expertly held the umbrella over both of them as they strolled, but after another hour of aimlessly wandering, chatting about nothing, her feet were getting tired, and the rain had picked up. She kept one hand in her pocket, touching the little box as if that would keep up her courage to follow through on her plan.

"Let's get a car," she suggested. They had two hours before they needed to be at the Lanesborough, but they could find a coffee shop or something close by.

Theodore looked up and down the street as if seeking something. "In a minute. Let's stretch our legs a bit."

They'd entered a street filled with little clothing stores, coffee shops and novelty places. The sidewalks were a little crowded with so many umbrellas, and he was having trouble keeping it over them. Drops of water were dripping off her raincoat, and the ends of her hair began hanging in wet clumps. Not exactly the look she wanted to be sporting during high tea.

"Are we lost?" She almost drew out her phone, when his hand tightened his grip on her fingers.

"Not lost. Just a bit early."

Early for what? She couldn't enter the Lanesborough looking like a drowned cat. "Well, I'm getting soaked. Let's stop into one of these shops."

"Alice." He stopped short. He swallowed hard. "We're good together, right?"

He suddenly looked so serious. She touched his arm. "We are," she said. "More than."

"And despite all this rain, you've liked living here? With me?"

She nodded. Why was he suddenly so nervous? She was the one about to propose.

Oh, crap. Was he having second thoughts about them? About her wanting to be here?

A couple brushed past them, and his umbrella tipped, sending a stream of water to splash near her feet. She jumped a little, an automatic reaction.

"Let's pop inside one of these shops." She turned to step up the concrete step into a candle shop when he pulled on her raincoat. They needed to talk.

"Not that one," he said. "Come with me."

The rain was now coming down with force. "Theodore, I'm like a drowned rat and—"

"Then, we should hurry." He looped his arm in hers and pulled her along.

"But a car…" She was practically jogging alongside him now. Her heart was hammering. What was going on with him?

"Not needed. Here." He stopped short. "I love you, Alice Crawford."

"I love you, too." Rain beat down on the umbrella.

"No, I need you to know. I *really* love you. Forever." His face searched hers, as he pulled her closer to him. That made her feel better. Okay, he wasn't having second thoughts.

A man jogged by, and his shoulder bumped Theodore, so his umbrella tilted again. A long stream of water cascaded down her back.

She yelped a little.

"Oy, mate," he said to the guy, and then spun her to face one of the shops. "Let's go in here."

She didn't bother to look at the large glass window to her right, just jogged up the small step and entered. A jingle went off and a plastic and nylon scent immediately hit her. As she shook water off her coat, she peered around. Blinked. What the devil?

Theodore closed the umbrella and dropped it in a stand near the door. "Surprise. Happy National BAE Day, Alice."

"You have got to be kidding me." Everywhere she looked

were shelves and shelves of bobblehead dolls. A slight breeze was blowing through the store making them all tilt and wobble their heads a little. There had to be a fan somewhere.

At the counter in the back, a bright neon pink sign on a yellow backdrop declared the shop's name: *BobblePop*. In other words, the ugliest thing she'd ever seen.

She faced him, searched his face for the hidden joke. "But it's not National Bobblehead day, it's…"

"Ah, you remembered."

"You brought up a lot of days that night." The evening they'd met. It felt like a hundred years ago, but yet like yesterday at the same time.

Theodore looked over her head and beamed a smile. "Oh, there she is."

A short roundish woman with gray hair scooted forward. "Ah, Mr. Gaston. Here we are. Here we are."

"Marge, thought we'd take a look around."

The woman gave him a small smile and dipped her chin. "Of course. You know the way."

Oh, my God. He must have been here a lot.

Alice looked up at him. His face was lit up like he won the lottery or something. He was honestly, genuinely happy to be there.

She could rally. She loved Theodore, and he clearly loved her… and bobbleheads? She would be the woman that Theodore needed at this moment. Be excited for him. Plus, the reprieve from the rain was welcomed. When they got to tea, the plan would be back on track.

She shook out the ends of her coat a little to stop the dripping, and took in a lungful of stinky air, trying not to cough. Time to channel her fun side—the one Theodore brought out in her. "Ah, so this is your hidden fetish." She bumped her shoulder against him.

He lifted a bobblehead doll of the Queen, who held a

scepter in her hand, held it up to his cheek. "She's pretty cute."

Alice reached for the bobblehead that she thought was Prince Philip. "Don't separate them."

"I'm afraid that's happened already," he sighed and put the Queen doll back.

Buzz kill. "How about this one?" She moved to a Taylor Swift bobblehead but didn't pick her up. "No wait. She's taken." Her rain boots squeaked on the floor as they slowly walked along the aisles.

"I prefer brunettes anyway. Like this one." He lifted a doll that Alice thought might resemble a supermodel from some magazine she'd recently seen.

"Well, if you get her, my celebrity out clause is this one." She grabbed the Henry Cavill bobblehead doll.

He gasped. "I thought you had a thing for gingers."

"Variety is the spice of life." She picked up a second doll— this one clearly David Beckham by the soccer ball at his feet. "In fact, I want two."

"Ah, cheating. That defies BAE Day." He slapped his chest.

She placed the dolls back on the shelf. "You'll always be my BAE. Does your photographic memory remember what you told me the first night we met?"

"Of course. That January 7 is National Bobblehead Day?"

She moved closer to him, swiping wet hair off her forehead. It was beginning to drip down the side of her neck now. "That January was your favorite month."

He tugged her into him. "I'm now declaring my favorite is June."

Her chest warmed. "Me, too. Let's call a car from here. Go to tea." She was done with the silly and wanted to move to something real. Plus, he was making her nervous. Or maybe it was all the eyes watching them as they walked among the bobbleheads.

"In a bit," he said.

"Please?" She arched an eyebrow. "I mean, I get you love —" she waved her hand around. "—this. But my surprise awaits."

"Yours isn't over yet." He leaned down and captured her lips for a quick kiss. "There's something I want to ask you." He knelt.

Oh no. His face was serious. He was on his knees. He'd been so nervous a few minutes ago. And it was National BAE Day. Outside this place he'd said he loved her. Forever. Was he going to…?

No. No. She couldn't, *wouldn't*, get engaged in a *bobblehead store*.

She was going to faint. "I need tea," she blurted out.

"Oh, love, I'll bring some right out for ya' then." Marge had been standing behind the counter but disappeared behind a curtain.

She'd meant she needed them to get to the Lanesborough where they'd do this thing properly. She hadn't spent half a month's salary for nothing. Not to mention enduring the upright sniffing of the clerk at Clairmont Diamonds—their unspoken message of *how the hell did you get in here?*—as she perused rings. How was she supposed to know she was supposed to make an appointment to spend money? She was shocked they hadn't asked for references before crossing the threshold.

"Alice, down here." She dropped her gaze to Theodore who was still kneeling on the floor. "The night we met was the best night of my life. Kiss a Ginger Day."

This was happening. "Mine, too. Are you going to…"

He gasped. "Who told you?"

Oh, my. There was nothing else to do. She got on her knees, too. "I mean… I'm guessing… And I do. I love you… I would love to… but…. tea…" Gah, she was rambling.

He chuckled. "Look." He cocked his head to the bottom shelf. There were two dolls there—one brunette and one redhead—their heads wobbling in sync. "Custom made. Theodore and Alice."

"Oh." She moved an envelope that was resting against the Theodore doll and picked him up. He held a calendar that read June with the 23rd circled in a heart. It was sweet. Romantic, when she really thought about it.

She looked up at Theodore, his blue eyes shining. She really did love this man. Her eyes pricked. "You're better looking."

"Of course, I am." He picked up the Alice doll. "She has something for you." She put the Theodore doll down and took the Alice version. It looked like her, standing in a red business suit—the color Theodore had declared she owned, holding a clipboard. And inside, tucked against her chest, was a ring.

Oh, my. There was no question now. He was planning to ask her to marry him.

He lifted out the ring, holding it up to her. It was a perfect solitary diamond in a platinum setting. Simple, but huge. "Alice Crawford, will you..."

He stopped when a rustling and clinking sounded behind him. "Ah, here we go. A nice cup of tea will warm you right up." Marge sat the tea service, a small pot and two cups on a tray, on the counter edge. Her eyes got wide. "Oh. Yes. Right. Well, I'll be in the back then." She quickly scooted out.

Theodore returned his gaze to her, smiling. "Best laid plans." He let his hand sink to his thigh, still holding the ring, and chuckled. Little crinkles formed around his eyes—his beautiful blue eyes that looked at her with so much love she didn't care where she was.

Her heart burst open with something new. Gratitude. It was an odd emotion to arise, as she knelt before Theodore, her hair wet and the damp seeping into her bones, holding a bobblehead doll. But she couldn't imagine being anywhere else. Because Theodore was there.

They'd met under the strangest circumstances. Survived a lot of secrets. She lost him. Then got him back. She got a whole new career, thanks to him. And she never, ever got sick of being with him. She was so lucky.

But so was he. That wasn't her ego talking. It was because they truly did fit like two gears meant to move something larger than they were.

"Wait." She set the doll down, and patted her pocket. "I was going to…" She reached in and pulled out the little box. She held it out to him. "I was going to do this over our afternoon tea, but…"

He took the box from her and stared at it. "You were?"

She nodded.

"You really did surprise me." He looked up at her. "You surprise me every day, and I wouldn't want it any other way." He put it on the shelf with the bobbleheads. "Mind if I go first?"

She slowly shook her head.

He held up the ring again. "Alice Crawford, will you be my wife?"

A giggle burst out of her throat, and she nodded vigorously. "Yes, Theodore, I will."

He slipped the ring on her finger, and she immediately stared at it. Her fingers touched the metal on either side. It was so beautiful and sparkly. It reminded her of Theodore's eyes.

She shot her gaze up. "My turn." She picked up the box and held it out to him. He cracked it open and grinned.

She drew in one long breath. "Theodore Gaston, the Fourth. This is me, in the bobblehead store, asking you to marry me."

"Yes, Alice Crawford. Anywhere. Anytime. Forever."

Her eyes pricked once more. He really was great with words. "It's inscribed." She pointed at the ring.

He pulled it out and held it up. *"Forever Kissing This Ginger."* His eyes shone with emotion.

She quickly took it and slipped it on his finger. He then rose, pulling her up with him. "One more present."

He bent over, picked up the large envelope that had been resting against the dolls, handing it to her. Inside was a document on stiff paper. Her hand flew to her mouth. "It's a certificate from the National Day Archives. Theodore and Alice Day."

She rolled her lips between her teeth, and her throat closed. "I love it," she managed to squeak out. She did, even more than the huge diamond on her left hand.

She rose up on tiptoes and planted a big kiss on his lips.

She was aware in the distance, a light clapping ensued. Other people had entered the store? And Marge had returned.

Theodore held her tight as he looked over at the five or six people in the store. "She said yes."

"Tea," Marge declared. "For everyone!" Murmurs followed. She hated to disappoint them, so they'd have one cup and then they'd head out.

Theodore leaned down and whispered in her ear. "Ready to get some proper tea? We can pick up the dolls later."

She gasped. "And leave them behind? Never."

He let out a long laugh. "Does this mean we get to celebrate National Bobblehead Day every year now?"

"Only if you want to."

"I'd rather celebrate our day. Forget the others. Except…"

She smiled up at him. "Kiss a Ginger Day? Every day."

Theodore grasped Alice's hand, holding it up to the light. "Mrs. Alice Gaston. I like the sound of that."

She smiled at up at him. "Even better? Mrs. Alice Craw-ford-Gaston *the first*."

"And the one and only." He bent his head and captured his lips. "Happy BAE Day," he said into her mouth.

"Happy Theodore and Alice Day."

Best day ever. Even if it started in a bobblehead store.

~The End~

Want to read a bonus epilogue to learn where Theodore and Alice landed a year later? Visit www.ElizabethSaFleur.com to read this and more bonus materials from many of her books.

ALSO BY ELIZABETH SAFLEUR

Sexy romcoms:

The Sassy Nanny Dilemma

It Was All The Pie's Fault

It Was All the Cat's Fault

It Was All the Daisy's Fault

For You, Anything

Kiss a Ginger Day

Kissing Frogs and Other Romantic Crimes

Steamy Contemporary romance:

Tough Luck

Tough Break

Tough Love

Short story collections:

Finally, Yours

Finally, His

Finally, Mine

Erotic romance with BDSM:

Elite

Holiday Ties

Untouchable

Perfect

Riptide

Lucky

Fearless

Invincible

Femme Domme:

The White House Gets A Spanking

Spanking the Senator

ABOUT THE AUTHOR

Elizabeth SaFleur writes award-winning, luscious romance from 28 wildlife-filled acres, is a certifiable tea snob, and is ruled by a 17 lb. Westie.

Never miss a new release by signing up for her email newsletter at her web site ElizabethSaFleur.com or join her private Facebook group, Elizabeth's Playroom.

Follow her on TikTok (@ElizabethSaFleurAuthor) and Instagram (@ElizabethLoveStory), too.